Twelve Stories

By

Frank L Kress

Introduction/Acknowledgments/Dedication

All of the stories are fictional, but each one was written specifically for someone; either as a source of inspiration or simply as entertainment, so basically each one has a purpose. Some were written a few years back and some are brand new so thematically, there is quite a range in the feel of each one. They are all written in the first person not only because I wanted to use different voices, but simply because it is a style that I enjoy as a writer as well as a reader.

As for the dedication, well, this book is dedicated to you. Since there will be those of you that I know, hopefully you can visit some old friends in these stories and for those new readers, I hope that you will find some to your liking. If you do, please let me know! And if you don't, you can let me know that too. My email address will be at the end of the book and I sincerely hope that you'll drop me a line. Your feedback is not only appreciated, it is critical. Plus, you may become one of the people that I base my next story on.

Top of the Ninth

I closed my eyes and remembered the words "Do me this last favor."

On a rainy Tuesday morning in July, Floyd Tendrick was driving down Range Road 76 on his way to Our Lady of Lourdes Catholic Church, wearing his usual Sunday suit and reeking of gin. He slammed on his brakes to avoid a rabbit (possibly imaginary) and flipped his 23 year old Chevy truck over. Floyd wasn't hurt, but he was terribly disappointed. He wanted to get a good seat at the church.

Less than a mile behind, Mrs. Gladys Fennerty, dressed in her funereal best and not wearing her tortoise shell glasses (the one that made her face look fat) plowed into the side of Floyd's truck. Luckily the owner was a safe distance away, on the side of the road taking a leak.

Due to poor visibility and the general excitement of a small town funeral, three more cars were added to the obstruction on the only road that led to the small Catholic Church, fifteen miles away. The hearse that held the remains of my cousin, Sicily Purtan, was stuck somewhere in the middle of the procession.

When the news came to Father Andrew and me via cell phone, I morbidly told the priest that my constantly tardy cousin had made our fifth grade teacher a prophet. In response to Father

Andrew's cocked eyebrow I said, "She always said that Sicily would be late for her own funeral."

"How's the eulogy coming, Gilly?" The priest asked, refusing to acknowledge my lame attempt at humor.

"Great." I said in a tone that meant the opposite. "This delay is a bit of a blessing."

"Don't worry, you'll get it." He said, patting me on the shoulder before briskly walking toward his quarters that lay to the right of the altar, leaving me alone in the sanctuary. I wished for a cigarette but I was too lazy to get up and go outside. I heaved a great breath of air and closed my eyes.

Setting the notebook down on the pew beside me, I looked at the rain cascading off the slanted stained glass windows. I shivered involuntarily and looked around the empty church. The painting of the Stations of the Cross depressed me, as they always did, and the ten wooden plaques with the carved words of the commandments made me smile ruefully. "Thou shalt have no other gods before me." I thought that I was doing fine with that one. "Thou shalt not create graven images." I thought about the wobbly ashtray I made in art class. I couldn't even draw. "Thou shalt not take the name of thy Lord God in vain." Goddam, I thought, I'm doing great! I quickly looked across to the opposite wall and lingered on the one about killing.

After a few moments I picked up the notebook again and read over the first few lines of the eulogy. My first eulogy. "My First Eulogy – by Gilbert A. Tennison." The title was meant to be a little joke and believe me; I needed all the levity that I could get my hands on. Most people thought that Sicily and I were the best of buddies but in a town where my choices were limited to my brooding cousin and the two overweight, acne splotched twins named Tim and Tom... anyway, I suppose Sicily was in the same boat as me. I know that I'm no great prize but if Mr. Barker, the guy who owned the gas station, had to give her eulogy, he probably could have come up with ten times more stuff than I could. Uncle Brett, Sicily's dad, had asked me to say the eulogy and I couldn't refuse. Like I said, when it came to friends, she was all I had and besides, I was with her when she died.

I looked through the walls of the church, ten miles away, to the bottom of a ravine where Sicily had been surrounded by the twisted metal of her Toyota Cressida. I touched the scar on my forehead and thought of how Sicily's face had looked... I quickly shook free of that thought and glanced down at the paper. I took out my pen to make a correction.

I changed, "Sicily *has* the nicest eyes," to "Sicily *had* the nicest eyes." As I scanned down the page, I saw that I had screwed up the tense half a dozen times. It hardly mattered because I didn't think most of the attendees would even listen and furthermore, just about everything I wrote were lies.

I lied because I didn't know her. I told a couple stories about how she and I had shared deep personal experiences with each other. We hadn't. Not until the very end anyway. I wrote about the time we saw a calf being born and put that poetic spin about the miracle of life in there. We did actually see the birth, but nothing about it moved us, not unless you include the movement of our stomachs as we witnessed the gory afterbirth ooze out after the sticky newborn calf. There was nothing in that, or in any other of my anecdotes that gave any kind of clue as to who Sicily was.

She was shy, reticent to the point of rudeness actually. She never smiled or laughed. She was late for school a lot, but that's not the kind of thing that people want to hear about someone who just died. None of the stuff I knew about her was noteworthy. Aside from her physical features, there was nothing to add and you can't write a eulogy about how someone was too tall (she was almost six feet) with stringy blonde hair (I don't think she ever washed it) and a bad posture (probably because she developed so early).

Sicily had huge boobs. There, let me jot that down. I'm sure her parents would love that.

Sicily had large breasts that she tried her damndest to hide. She slouched all the time, trying to veil her bosom within the bowl of her thick arms and her broad, overhanging shoulders. So aside from her hooters, she was invisible. She never spoke to anybody unless she had to and she never did anything crazy or wonderful or wicked so she was just this anonymous moose. Her good qualities (if she had any) were never thrust into prominence (just like her boobs).

She left town right after graduation to go to some art college in Edmonton and when she was gone, I thought I'd seen the last of her. I was leaving myself, having earned a full ride to the University of Nebraska (baseball scholarship – big whoop. In Alberta, the kid who scores two goals in his pee-wee hockey game is a bigger hero than someone who hit 27 home runs. By the way, that's 27 home runs in a 35 game schedule. Ahem.)

Anyway, when Sicily suddenly appeared back in town and right at my door, I was more than a little shocked. She never came over on her own volition. Previously, our time together was due to the mandate set by our respective parents. "You kids need to have fun! Being alone all the time isn't normal!" Pearls of wisdom, mom and dad, absolute pearls. Maybe they should have realized that living in a tiny hamlet, hours away from civilization wasn't normal. Maybe trying to get two completely different people to hang out without saying a word to each other for hours on end wasn't normal. Trying to force Sicily and I into becoming friends, when we had known each other all our lives, wasn't the least bit normal. I spent most of my time with the baseball team that was an amalgamation of kids from farms in a two hundred mile radius and Sicily spent her time... I have no idea what she spent her time with because, as I've been trying most painfully to get across, we weren't friends.

So Sicily showed up at the door and I was at a loss. She said that she needed to talk and with a blank expression I followed her to the car and we went for a drive. After a few minutes of stoic silence she said, "I have cancer."

She had lymphatic cancer. The terminal, abandon ye all hope, put your house in order kind of cancer. She was 19 years old, 2 months older than I, and she was riddled with cancer. Her lymph nodes spread the disease in no time and she had it in her lungs, though she never smoked, in her liver, though she never drank and in her ovaries, though she never ...

One time, when we were 14 years old, she let me feel her breasts. I had to practicallybeg her and she made me stop long before I wanted to. When we were 17, we French kissed and she let me put my hand under my shirt. We were first cousins, but it wasn't the incestuous aspect that bothered her. It was the sexual part of it. She didn't have any discernible urges when it came to sex. I only know that because after we stopped kissing, she said she thought she was pheromone deficient.

As she drove, she confessed that she was scared of dying and I only nodded in reply. She told me that she wasn't going to seek treatment and I stared out the window, not looking at her. She said that wasn't any point. She said... she said more in that drive than she had ever said in her entire life.

"Gilly!" The priest's angry voice caught me off guard and I looked around wildly, seeing his angry face close by. "You can't smoke in here!"

I looked down at the cigarette that I was holding and had no recollection of ever lighting it. I immediately snubbed it out on the sole of my shoe. Father Andrew shook his head slowly and he certainly would have harangued me further if it were not for the present circumstances. "Besides," he said softly, "What would the scouts say if they saw you smoking?"

"Nothing," I said as I put the butt in the pocket of my blazer. "I'm going to Nebraska."

"Still, you can't smoke and hit 25 home runs a year."

"27." I said.

"And how many RBI's?" He asked with a sweet smile.

I knew that he, like everyone else around, cared nothing about baseball and was only asking to be nice. "Oh, who cares. Little Timmy scored a goal against the Drayton Valley Whoevers."

"Did he now?" He grinned. "Well good for him."

I narrowed my eyes at him and he said, "Don't be bitter, Gilly. We're all proud of you."

I nodded sullenly and threw the notebook down beside me.

"It's difficult, isn't it?" Father Andrew asked softly.

Yes, it was difficult. Truth was a stray dog and no matter how hard I tried to get it to go away, it slunk back, ready to nip me.

"You two were close, weren't you?"

I thought about the Toyota Cressida wrapped around a tree and the dented steering wheel. I thought about her last words and about the favor she asked me to do. I could feel tears in my eyes. I shook my head. "No. We weren't close."

"Still." He said after a lengthy pause. "She was your cousin."

I wiped my eyes and looked away. My gaze went right to the plaque on the wall. Right at the sixth commandment.

"Words to live by, right?" I said, feeling the words choke in my throat.

"Yes," He replied in a quiet voice, "They are."

I reached into my pocket for the cigarette and he put his hand on top of mine. "Gilly, you can't do that."

I looked down at my hand again and whispered, "Shit."

"Gilly!"

I turned to face him, "We weren't close!"

"Yes, but…"

"I screwed up, Father."

He looked at me with a concerned expression. "You can tell me whatever is on your mind."

I smiled, "You want me to have confession?"

He smile back, "Sure."

"OK. You first."

He shook his head. "That's not the way it works."

"How come? You don't have any sins to confess?"

"Not to you, Gilly."

I let out a harsh laugh.

"But you can talk to me, son."

"C'mon Father, just one. Just tell me one little sin of yours to get the ball rolling."

He shook his head.

"Fine, then I'm not telling either."

"OK." He said.

I stared at him, "How's that for love and forgiveness!"

"Are you asking me for forgiveness?"

I looked away and didn't reply.

"Gilly." He said in a stern voice. "What do you want me to forgive?"

"Nothing." I said without looking at him.

He sat down on the end of the pew across the aisle from me. After a few seconds he said, "Talk to me."

I took a deep breath. "Sicily had cancer."

After a lengthy pause he nodded, "I know."

I looked at him questioningly and he gave his shoulders a little shrug. "Sicily came to see me when she came back from Edmonton."

"She was terrified." I said, standing up and walking a few feet away. "She told me, Father. She told me how scared she was. She told me about her dreams, about being an artist, about seeing the world! She told me secrets and she kept on telling me things that I could have never guessed..." I let out a sob but the priest didn't say a word.

"She told me that she didn't want to waste away! She said that she couldn't face the pain! She was crying and swerving all over the road, heading straight for Duncan Ravine. She was hysterical."

Father Andrew's gentle voice seemed to come from the air. "And she crashed."

"No." I said, shaking my head. "She stopped the car and told me to get out. She unhooked her seatbelt and told me to get out of the car."

I turned toward the cross and let out another sob. "I didn't want to. She had to yell at me, she had to threaten to kill us both if I didn't. So I got out. I stood on the side of the road and the tires squealed and gravel flew up." I touched the scar on my forehead absentmindedly. "She went right over the edge, into the ravine. I heard the crash and I saw the top of that big polar tree sway when she hit it."

The priest's voice was contemplative. "You weren't even in the car."

"No. I ran toward her as soon as I heard the crash and I saw the car, with smoke pouring out of the smashed hood. She was bent over the steering wheel and there was blood all over her face. I tore open the door..."

"She was dead."

I shook my head, "No. She looked at me, Father. And with all the blood... it covered it face, it was like she was crying two kinds of tears. She fell out of the car at my feet and cried, telling me that I had to help her. She begged me to help her." I turned around and faced the priest. "I thought that she wanted me to take her to the hospital but she stood up and leaned against the car, feeling her way to the trunk. She was wobbling so badly and she almost fell but she got out the..."

After a couple seconds he asked, "What did she get?"

"The tire iron. She wanted me to hit her with it. She wanted me to kill her."

The priest stared at me wordlessly.

"I told her that I couldn't but she begged me! She got on her knees and looked up at me and I felt... God, I don't know! Pity? Mercy?" I took a deep breath. "She kept looking at me, crying, pleading. Her forehead was a red bull's eye, right in the strike zone. I took my stance... I lined up perfectly. My coach would have been proud." I swallowed back a lump and took a breath before whispering, "Then I did it."

"Then, after you hit her?"

I yelled, "Then I puked and you would have too! God, the sound of it! The feel of it and the way she flew back." I closed my eyes and the image was before me. "You couldn't even see her face, Father. There was nothing left." I felt tears course down my cheeks. "I puked and then I threw the tire iron as far as I could. Then I think I passed out." I showed him the deep red scratch on my forearm. "I fell against the jagged metal of the hood." I wiped the tears away with my left hand and said, "I put her back in the car, with her head against the dented steering wheel and left her..." I swallowed back the sob that I could feel in my throat and stared at the priest. "So what do I do now, Father? What do I do now?"

We stared at each other for half a minute and then he stood up and took me in his arms. I hugged him fiercely and he let me cry against his shoulder. When my tears were spent he gripped my shoulders and held me at arm's length. "What you'll do is, you'll say your eulogy, go to Nebraska and become a baseball star. You'll live each moment like it's the top of the ninth."

I smiled thinly, "You mean the bottom of the ninth."

He shook his head, "No, the top. When you've given everything you've got, the world still gets one more at bat against you. You have to swing like hell, even when you know that life gets to take another shot at you."

When my tears had dried, Father Andrew left me alone and I sat down in the back pew and tore out the pages in my notebook. I wrote a new eulogy, one where I admitted that I never knew Sicily the way people thought I did. I wrote about her dreams and her fears and even her bravery. When the time came, I wept as I spoke the words out loud.

A few weeks later I went to Nebraska but I never even tried out for the team. I lost my scholarship because I couldn't stand at the plate anymore. Might Gilly had struck out.

If Sicily had lived, I wouldn't have given her a second thought. As it is, I think about her all the time and I think of her with hate and with anger but also with pity. Sicily knelt down at the top of the ninth and begged me to swing and now I'm there too, but I keep reminding myself that I can't kneel down. I know that I have to stand at the plate and take what's thrown, knowing that whatever I do, good or bad, life will still get one more shot at me.

Fielding

Highway 33 was dark and I slid down in the seat and leaned my head back. I was driving about 20 clicks over the speed limit and I could feel myself getting sleepier by the mile. It was the middle of September so the window was halfway down and the wind was a degree or two below just being cool and I kept the radio on loud. The blue lights on the dashboard read 11:45pm. I had been on the road for the past five hours and I was still an hour away from home.

On either side of the highway were trees and fields and the occasional farm house. I hadn't seen another set of headlights in the last half hour. I yawned, for what seemed like the fiftieth time and lit another cigarette just to have something to do.

I saw the flash of light out of the corner of my left eye. I could have sworn it was a strobe light but it quickly disappeared behind a small forest of trees. I could feel my breath quicken because I thought about lonely drivers on even lonelier highways and how it's usually those sad bastards that end up seeing a UFO. Another flash of light ahead and to the left and that time I took my foot off the gas and leaned forward, peering into the night.

The car coasted down to seventy, sixty, fifty, forty and then I saw the light again. I turned off the radio because I thought I heard something. I pressed the button and the window glided all the way down. At that slow speed, the breeze was warmer and filled the car with an autumn smell. The light flashed again and I could hear music coming across an open field.

I slowed the car to a crawl and watched the white light shoot up to the sky, illuminating a stand of trees.   The music got louder and it wasn't recorded... it was live and loud and distorted.   I saw the first car that was parked on the side of the highway and then as my eyes adjusted to the darkness, I saw more vehicles parked alongside.   As I cruised past them, I estimated around 30 vehicles. I pulled in beside the last one and shut the car off.   Just to make sure of my surroundings, I looked around for some kind of community hall, even though I travelled that road once every couple months and thought that I knew it like the back of my hand.

When I got out of the car, the music was even louder and I could hear voices and cheers added to the sounds just beyond the trees. I started to walk through the chest-high grasses that bent and waved in the breeze, finding a pathway of sorts off to the left.   The "path" was new and obviously temporary since the long grasses were still intact.   The music reached a crescendo and then stopped, immediately followed by applause, cheers and shouts.   A garbled male voice spoke into a microphone and I could only catch one or two words before the music started again.   I hurried forward and after reaching the edge of the trees I saw the stage, lit up for a concert and a quartet of musicians playing.   A crowd of about 100 to 150 people were in front of the stage, dancing, singing or milling around, as all crowds tend to do.

I walked over to a young couple who swayed back and forth to the music and when I was beside them, they smiled and nodded in greeting.   I leaned in closer and spoke in a loud voice against the music, "What's going on?"

The girl leaned in my direction and shouted, "It's a concert!"

I smiled and nodded, "I see that!   But out here in the middle of nowhere?"

She shrugged her shoulders and grinned, "I know! It's crazy, right? We saw the lights from the highway and came to check it out!"

I looked around at the audience and noted that most of the crowd was in their teens or twenties. There were a few older faces doted throughout the group as well, but they did not seem as interested in the music. I figured that they were only there to see what the commotion was all about and as if in confirmation of that, two separate couples who I gauged to be in their fifties walked away down the same path that I had come by. Obviously they weren't fans of the rock music being belched out of the Marshall stacks.

After watching them depart, I turned back to the stage and watched the band play. They were all fully in character, playing like they were headlining at Madison Square Garden. The music was rough and edgy, a cross between a hundred different bands on college radio – nothing original, but not bad at all. It made me think about the bands that I used to cover when I did some part time writing for a local music magazine. None of the local bands that I covered ever made it big and I didn't think the band on the stage would either, but to look at them and hear the passion in their playing, you knew that they would never believe in failure or obscurity. The name on the bass drum was "The Start Overs" and the letters seemed in jeopardy of falling off due to the ferocity with which the drummer plied his trade.

The lead singer was a slim younger guy, dressed in a t-shirt and tight, shiny pants. His head thrummed back and forth as he melodically growled into the microphone. He leaned on the microphone stand when it came time in the song to try some crooning and the way he stared out into the crowd told me that he played the front man role consummately, playing all the seductive tricks in the book. The guitarist was another typecast: a tall, skinny guy feverishly picking on a Les Paul that hung lower than his hips. His impossibly long arms reached just above his knees to slide along the frets. His chin was on his chest and his hair obscured his face except for the scowl that seemed permanently etched onto his mouth. The bass player was a sexy looking girl, all long limbed and hair, marching across the stage from one pedestal to another, staying in one spot only long enough for someone in the crowd to fall in love. The manic drummer was bald. I never saw a head thrash as wildly on any musician before. I envisioned long years of chiropractic care in his future.

When the song ended, the singer looked over the crowd and mumbled a simple "thanks for coming out." And then the rest of the band all exited stage left, going down a short flight of stairs and disappearing behind the stage. The lights went out except for a single spot light on the singer's microphone stand. The crowd took this as a cue to scream for an encore. The cheering grew louder and louder and then reached a wild climax when the lead guitarist came back on stage carrying an acoustic guitar. He walked over to the microphone and said, "OK, but this is absolutely the last one tonight." A girl who was standing nearby came over and leaned close to me, "They've come on for four encores already!"

I only nodded in reply because when I looked back to the stage, the guitarist was seated on a stool and what appeared to be a roadie was lowering one of the microphone stands to the level of the guitar. The guitarist addressed the crowd again, "This is the first song I ever wrote and I guess it kind of suits the occasion. It's called, "Under the Stars."" The crowd cheered again and then slowly fell silent as the guitarist played the opening chords of his song.

I stood entranced by the sweetness of the simple music coming from the stage. It was a rich, earthly sound that seemed to blossom in the night air and when the guitarist began to sing the first words of the ballad, I found myself swaying along to the music, forgetting the long drive, the strangeness of the venue and the fact that my right hand was being held by the strange girl beside me. I looked over at her and we both were smiling. I gave her hand a squeeze and then turned my attention back to the stage and the almost hypnotic song.

"I was always alone, under the stars; I was always in pain, under the stars." The guitarist played the bridge as a short instrumental and with only the one light shining on him; I could look up and see the subject of his song gazing back down on him and on all of us. As I listened and watched the stars, I felt the weight of years falling away and I remembered all the dark and smoky clubs and the now nameless and faceless bands that I had watched and written of and even loved all glide behind my eyes. "I was always a fool, under the stars; I was always in tears, under the stars."

The music drifted to a soft close and the guitarist ended his song a cappella with the last lyrics, "I was always in love, under the stars." He mouthed the words, "Thank you" and stood up just as the lone light was turned off and the stage went black.   The crowd applauded and cheered but it was obvious that the band was done for the night.   The cheers went on for maybe a minute longer and then like a radio being turned down, it slowly came to an end and the crowd could be heard talking and laughing together. Some turned to go, some milled around and I turned to the girl and said, "I wish I had arrived sooner."

She had a beaming smile, "They played for three hours, pretty much non-stop."

"Wow," I said, "That's quite the set."

"Well, it's quite the gig, don't you think?"

"No kidding! Have you heard them before?"

She laughed, "I'm sort of the unofficial fan club president. I've been friends with them all for years."

"Is this their farm or something? Do they play here all the time?"

She shook her head, "No. It's... well, it's complicated.   Do you want to meet them?"

I replied, "Do you think they'd let me interview them?"

She stared at me for a second, "Are you a reporter?"

I smiled, a little overcome by her penetrating stare. "Retired. I used to write for *Tin Plated Tunes*. It was a music magazine..."

She cut me off, "I used to love *Tin Plated*!   And yeah, of course you can interview them! " She gave me a slanted grin, "What's your name?"

After I told her she beamed, "I've read your stuff!"

I smiled, "Bullshit."

She shook her head, "I'm serious! I like your writing!"

"So you're the one!"

She laughed, "That's me, your one and only fan. I'm Celine."

"Nice to meet you, Celine." I said, "Let me run back to the car and grab a notepad. I'll meet you back here, OK?"

She nodded, "For sure, I'll go tell them and then I'll meet you!"

I quickly walked down the path toward my car, not feeling remotely sleepy anymore. I got to the car and rummaged around in the glove box for the notepad and pen that I always kept handy and after closing the door I paused to take note of the expressions and demeanors of the people leaving. Every single one of them seemed pleased with what they had just experienced. A few of them were holding CD's and T-shirts that were obviously on sale somewhere back near the stage. There were those who arrived alone but left with new friends and there were a few families, with small children in tow – dancing and singing out loud, ecstatic because not only had they just seen a concert, but were allowed up way past their bedtimes. There were couples who held hands or walked with their arms around their partner's waists. Most everyone was smiling and some were laughing and no one looked tired or bored.

There were a few stragglers that I passed on the way back and I spotted Celine standing by the stage. She got on her tip toes to see over the heads of some people who were standing around her and waved to me. I waved back and politely waited for her to finish speaking to the other people.

"And don't forget to pick up a CD from the table. Oh, and they're playing again next Friday, at "The Pendulum on 124th street."

The group drifted away and Celine took hold of my hand and led me around the stage, past a couple pick-ups and one flat-bed truck. A newer travel trailer was parked behind them and we went up to the door and Celine knocked once but didn't wait for a reply before she opened the door. She leaned inside and presented me with a flourish, "And here he is!"

The drummer was sitting at the dinette table and looked up at me with a sneer, "And who the fuck is he?"

Celine snapped back, "A music writer you dumb ass. Someone who actually wants to listen to the stupid shit that comes out of your mouth."

The drummer gave a shrug and leaned back, taking a long drink of his beer without his eyes leaving me. Across from him sat the bass player and next to her was a guy with long hair and wearing a Slayer t-shirt, smoking a joint. I recognized the lead singer, sitting on the loveseat with a beautiful girl on his lap. I looked around for someplace to sit and another guy who was sitting in a recliner stood up, "You can sit here." He reached down and picked up his beer and as he walked toward the door he said, "I'm gonna go find Rob."

I sat down and took out my notepad and as my pen was poised, Celine brought me a beer, which I accepted with a smile. I introduced myself and told them how much I enjoyed their sound and expressed regret for coming so late to the show. Each of the band members told me their names and just as Emilio, the lead singer, finished introducing himself, the trailer door opened and the lead guitarist stepped inside and sat down on the loveseat, next to the singer. He gave me a friendly smile and said his name was Rob.

I knew that if my first questions were about the strange concert venue I would be marginalizing their music so we talked about musical influences (the usual eclectic mix, ranging from The Ramones to Bjork), how the band first formed, their thoughts on the local music scene and the industry itself. Emilio and Jennifer (the bass player) answered most of the questions. Troy (the drummer) added a few grunts at key moments but Rob sat silently, politely listening to his band mate's responses.

I took notes throughout and then gave them all a meek smile, "OK, I have to ask… what's up with the countryside concert?"

Jennifer laughed, "I was wondering when you were going to get to that! Anyway, that's Rob's baby... we should let him answer."

Rob shook his head with a smile, "You can answer as well as I can. Start with the rules."

Jennifer said, "Ah yes, the rules!" I looked over to her with an encouraging smile and she began, "OK, so the rules are this: One, you can't tell anyone. The rule is that it has to be super secret."

Emilio interjected, "You can tell one person that's not in the band. That's it."

Jennifer said, "That's not entirely true, when we started, no one was supposed to know."

Rob nodded but remained silent so Jennifer continued, "Anyway, the point is that no one is supposed to know. It's supposed to be spontaneous. Once people show up, they can call or text people to come see... in fact, that's encouraged. One day we'll be fielding..." She paused and looked at me, "That's what it's called by the way. Fielding. Named after our guitarist, Rob Fielding... but also because it's in a field. Duh!" I chuckled and she went on, "So anyway, one night we'll be fielding and thousands of people will just show up!"

Troy cut in, "That's a rule too, about the size..."

Jennifer shot him a scowl and said, "We're not there yet! Rule number two, the show has to be more than thirty miles out of town."

Troy interrupted again, "And you have to get permission from the owner of the land otherwise they'll turn a fucking shotgun on you like they did in the spring!"

Jennifer laughed, "That really isn't a rule, it's more like common sense. And it wasn't the farmer that tried to shoot us, it was his wife. He never told her that he agreed to let us set up in the middle of his wheat field." Everyone laughed at that. "Rule number three is that you have to do a full set, even if nobody shows. Even if you're just playing to the cows, you can't cut the show short."

Emilio said, "And you have to play it straight. No talking in between songs, no stopping if you fuck up a chord or break a string. You have to keep going just as if you were playing in a stadium full of people." Rob gave an approving nod.

Jennifer smiled, "The point is that it's a real concert. So to Troy's point, you have to make sure that there is enough room for a decent size crowd, plus parking."

Emilio said, "That's not really a rule either, that's logistics."

Jennifer shrugged, "Fair enough."

I asked, "You mention logistics… I imagine that there's a fair bit of work that goes into just setting up one show."

Emilio nodded, "No shit. Obviously we work off generators so renting those has to be done in advance, plus there's finding a location, which ties in to rule number four. It can't be at the same place twice." He noticed that Troy was about to say something so he quickly added, "Or at least not the same place twice in a row."

Troy nodded and Emilio turned back to me, "We do this twice a year. Once in the spring and once in the fall, usually after the harvest."

Troy snickered, "After the harvest. Two years ago none of us knew what that fuck that meant! Now we know the lingo about harvesting and shit. Rob turned us into fucking farmers!"

Rob smiled and Jennifer said, "So before you ask, this was our sixth show. We started two years ago. And before you ask about this too, no, we aren't the only ones doing this. We're starting a whole new thing. As far as I know, there are two other bands that have done it…" she grinned, "They just aren't as good at it as we are."

I turned to Rob, who so far hadn't said a thing, "So obviously Fielding is a pretty big project. Plus it must be expensive… renting the generators, getting the vehicles, it's like going on tour… for one night."

Jennifer answered, "It is. It's a commitment. The band has some good friends..." she looked at Celine and smiled, "And they help us out with the set up and manning the tables. And we do recoup some from merch... we usually sell all our stuff after one show like this. I guess people want to give something back for the free concert." She asked Celine, "How did we do tonight?"

Celine smiled, "I have one solitary t-shirt left." She looked at me with a smile, "Which I saved for you." Then she addressed the room in general, "But we sold every single CD and DVD from the last concert." She turned to me again, "My cousin Bart always films the shows. Plus he makes special tour shirts for every time we go Fielding. It has the date and the latitude and longitude on it."

Troy said, "We stole that idea from The Bash Brothers. (A local band that I was familiar with). They did that after their first show this spring."

Celine scowled at him, looking like a fierce lioness. "They stole that from Bart. Bart did that last year and I have the t-shirt to prove it."

Troy didn't reply, probably because he knew she was right. Jennifer quickly said, "Anyway, if we treat it like a "happening", which it really is, we make the money back. People are more willing to shell out if they feel like they were a part of something big. But we aren't doing it to get rich anyway."

I cleared my throat and I felt everyone's eyes on me but I turned to Rob again. "That kind of begs the question though... I mean, don't get me wrong, I think this is one of the coolest things I've ever seen. It's completely fucking radical. But I know how much work goes into setting this kind of thing up and I applaud your commitment to it... but I have to ask, is the juice worth the squeeze? Is it really worth it? Basically... why do it?"

Everyone seemed to be waiting for Rob to reply but he only gave me an enigmatic smile. When he sensed that no one was going to speak until he answered, he rubbed the bridge of nose and then stood up, "Let's get a breath of fresh air."

I let him pass and then I stood up and followed him out of the trailer. He didn't turn around to wait for me. He walked past the stage and into the field, toward the highway and I stayed a couple steps behind him. His pace slowed and eventually he stopped, turned around and said, "Do you have a smoke?"

I shook one out of my pack and handed it to him. He fished a lighter out of his pocket and lit it and then exhaled a long stream of smoke toward the sky. He looked at me with a sly smile, "Are you really going to get a magazine to publish this?"

I nodded, "Yeah, I think it's a good story."

He smiled, "Yeah, me too." He took another deep drag off the cigarette and gave me another sidelong smile, "I was driving back from Dawson Creek a few years ago. It was the middle of the night and I guess I was pretty bagged, you know what it's like driving alone when all you want to do is sleep."

I nodded and he continued, "I thought, what if I go around the next bend and all of a sudden I see a concert going on in the middle of nowhere? Like a million dollar light show and hear music blaring... like a full blown U2 concert going on where no one in the world would ever expect to see it?" He grinned at me and I smiled back as I envisioned the scene he had described. "I guess I've always had a thing for secret places... hidden rooms and underground catacombs... things that are hidden from view but hold all these incredible treasures. That's what I equate it to. In a way it's like the Rolling Stones going to this crummy dive and jumping on stage and kicking out a few songs for the dozen or so people that happened to be there that night. Holy shit, those people would remember that for the rest of their lives!" He laughed, "Or shit, I dunno, like running into Stephen King at a coffee house and he hands you this hand written manuscript and says, "Here, this one is just for you. Enjoy it."

I said, "Isn't it more like Stephen King going into the woods and burying that manuscript without letting anyone read it?"

Rob was silent for a moment and said, "You may be right... it probably is more like that. But the thing is, just imagine if you were out in those woods and came across that hole and you yank out the manuscript? How much cooler would that be?"

I had to nod in agreement.

He said, "I guess there's the rub... we can play with the ultimate goal of getting rich and famous and we can also jump onto a stage and play for a few devoted fans, but when we go out here and play our fucking guts out for random people, it just means that much more. We go through all the trouble of setting up the stage and getting everything going, like you said, essentially setting up for a one night tour and we run the risk of absolutely no one showing up. We're putting it all out there with the chance that not one person will hear us play. To me, it's like we're offering a gift to anyone willing to accept it, but knowing that there's the very real possibility that no one will be there to accept it. But imagine if just one guy shows up... and we play a full set just for him... that guy would feel like the center of the fucking universe."

I smiled as I pictured that very thing happening. "So what does happen if nobody shows up?"

He smiled, "You just described our very first time Fielding. We put it all together and wouldn't you know it... no one came. I mean, it was my fault. I picked a shitty spot that was too far from the highway and just our luck it got cold and the wind started to howl and when we finished a song... it was dead silence. I mean, DEAD silent. Until I shouted, "One, two, three, four!" and then we kicked into the next song. When it was over, when we played for almost two hours without a break and the only applause was the wind in the trees... it was almost a religious experience. It was like we were only playing for the sake of the music, or playing for the trees and the grass." His smile widened, "It was like we were playing for God."

I returned the smile and asked, "So are you disappointed now when people actually show up?"

He laughed, "It's funny you should ask that. Like I said, the first time was surreal and mystical. We didn't really talk about it but you could tell that everyone, even Troy, was blown away by it. It was so spiritual and raw and it made me feel like an ancient Israelite building an altar way out in the desert, all by himself and then sacrificing a sheep on it. I know that sounds fucked up, but when we did the second show, we were all kind of hoping that it would go the same way as the first one so when the first few people showed up, I'm sure we all felt a little disappointed. But then we got into the spirit of the thing and more and more people showed up and it was like, pardon the expression but I'm stretching the metaphor a bit here, it was like manna from Heaven. We think about three thousand people were at that show."

I whistled and he nodded, "I know, right? Crazy shit. So yeah, maybe that helps explain the whys a bit, yeah?"

I said, "It does."

After a few minutes of silently looking up at the stars I asked, "How do you feel about other bands copying you?"

He laughed, "I think it's fucking awesome! I hope we're starting a trend! I keep hope alive that one night I'll be driving down the highway and I'll get to see a full blown U2 concert all by myself!"

I joined in the laughter and then his mysterious smile reappeared. "Can I trust you with something?"

I shrugged, "Sure."

"I mean, can I trust you not to include something in your article? Even beyond that, something that you won't tell the rest of the guys?"

I hoped that I wasn't agreeing to something that would hurt my chances of publishing the article but I said, "Absolutely."

He looked me in the eyes for a good five seconds, as if testing to make sure I was being forthright and then, apparently satisfied, he said, "This is my last show. I'm quitting the band."

I felt like I had been struck. "Why?"

He shrugged, "It's time. I'm twenty seven years old and I'm no Keith Richards… I always knew I had a limited shelf life as a rock and roll God." He laughed. "And I'm just the guitar player, they can replace me." He sighed, "I accepted a job in Toronto. As an accountant." He gave me a hard stare but his eyes were full of laughter, "Don't judge me. I know I'm a sellout. It's just that I want the band to carry on and keep Fielding. It's a cool thing to be a pioneer, no matter what it's for. I hope they don't give it up."

I said, "They seem pretty committed to it."

He nodded, "Yeah, I think so too." He paused, "So you won't say anything right?"

I offered him my hand and he shook it. "I promise." I said.

He stubbed out the cigarette into the dewy soil and stuck his hands in his pockets. I watched as he walked through the path back toward the stage and then I turned around and went back to my car. Once inside, I turned on the heater to ward off the chilly air and warmed my hands over the vent. I took a deep breath and turned the car around and headed back home.

The article was published a few weeks later and over the coming months I heard that a few more bands had taken up Fielding but even though I continued to travel, I was never fortunate enough to see another show. But that doesn't stop from me from casting a hopeful gaze around each bend, looking for colored lights and listening for music being played as an offering to God.

Phangs on Knecks

(The Obligatory Vampire Story)

Episode One

"Tastes like Chicken"

The new guy was a farmer. He was even wearing overalls. He looked to be in his mid-twenties, with an unruly shock of dirty blonde hair and a scruffy beard. He smelled like chickens.

He was lying on his back on my kitchen floor. His skin was white because he had been drained of all his blood. The wound at his neck was slowly fading and when his eyes began to flutter open, he saw my roommate Skeeter and me leaning over him. He looked distressed and rightly so, since Skeeter and I had just killed him.

"What's going on?" He asked in a shaky voice.

"Don't panic." I replied helpfully as Skeeter leaned closer in a way as to induce even more panic.

"What's happening?" The guy asked, his eyes flicking wildly between Skeeter and I.

I offered him a coffee mug which contained blood. "Here, drink this."

He struggled to get up but he was far too weak. "Why can't I move?"

Skeeter spoke in a loud, slow voice, "YOU CAN'T MOVE BECAUSE YOU'VE BEEN DRAINED OF ALL YOUR BLOOD!" He pointed to me and then back to himself, "WE'RE VAMPIRES!" When the new guy's face registered terror he added, "BUT THERE IS NOTHING TO FEAR!"

I said, "He's not deaf Skeeter."

"Sorry," Skeeter said in a quiet voice, "This is my first newbie."

"Go sit down," I said, "You're freaking him out."

Skeeter sat down on one of the kitchen chairs, still staring at the new guy with a curious yet excited expression.

I held the mug out again, "Once you drink this, you'll feel a lot better. You'll be able to move."

He tried to lift his arm but after managing a few inches, it feebly dropped to his side again. I put an arm around his shoulder and lifted him up a bit, supporting him as I held the mug to his lips. Once he got a whiff of the blood, his eyes widened and his whole head lurched toward the mug. After one large gulp he had the strength to grab the mug out of my hands and then he drained the whole thing. It's always a gruesome sight, seeing someone drink blood, but it's even worse when they're jonesing for a drink like this guy obviously was because they're frenzied and wild eyed and forget to wipe their chins. It's pretty gross.

Immediately after drinking every last drop he tried to stick his tongue in the mug to lick the dregs. When he got all he could he mumbled, "That was blood."

I nodded.

"I feel better."

"Told you." Skeeter said smugly.

He held the mug out to me, "Can I have some more?"

I took the mug from him and said, "Trust me, you don't want more. In fact, you better lay back for a second."

Skeeter smiled, "Wait for it."

A few seconds went by and then the new guy's eyes rolled up and he fell back onto the floor, passed out. It always happens after a blood chug a lug... human blood is kind of like a good glass of port, it's meant for sipping. We knew that he would be out for at least an hour so Skeeter and I hoisted him over to the couch and plopped him down in between us while we played Halo 3.

So I'm sure you've gathered the basics here: I'm a vampire.

Shocking, right? I suppose it isn't really because nowadays there are like 14 TV shows, 537,255 separate novels and 10,398 movies about vampires. We're a hot trend. But like any trend, there's a lot of fiction out there about us. If you're a big vampire fan then I should warn you... you're going to be disappointed. The truth is always a let down.

An hour later, the new guy began to stir and woke up to Skeeter threatening my player, "You're gonna die you son of a bitch, you're gonna die a horrible death!"

He might have thought that Skeeter was addressing him because he let out a little groan. Skeeter hit pause and turned to him, "Hi."

The new guy then turned to me.

"Hi." I said.

He jumped up and made a break for the door but Skeeter and I gang tackled him before he made it very far. He was struggling under our combined weight and since Skeeter and I aren't exactly highly skilled in any combative aspects, it took us a few seconds to subdue him by applying a kind of double half nelson and choke hold.

He continued to struggle and I shouted, "Look! We're not going to hurt you! We just want to help!"

After a couple more thrashing attempts to dislodge us he finally stopped, went limp and mumbled into the carpet, "Let me up. I won't run."

I nodded to Skeeter and we both rolled off him, letting the new guy get to his feet.

"So," he said after a long appraising look. "You guys are vampires."

I nodded, "That's right."

"Bullshit."

I smiled, "That's a reasonable response."

"Vampires don't exist."

My smile remained, "That's also a reasonable theory."

"Seriously," Albert said with his hands raised, "What do you guys want with me?"

"We only want to help you out, give you some information and let you be on your way."

"Why?"

"Well, when I became a vampire, no one told me anything. I was on my own and figuring this stuff out without any help isn't any kind of fun."

"Seriously," He said again, "This is a joke, right? You drugged me."

I shook my head, "No joke. And we didn't drug you."

"What did I drink? What was in that mug?"

"Blood."

"Bullshit."

I smiled again, "I know it's a lot to try to take in all at once."

"Prove it."

"Prove what?"

"Prove that you're a vampire."

"OK, but don't freak out." I went into the kitchen and came back with a carving knife.

He looked petrified, "What are you going to do?"

"Don't worry, I'm going to use this on me, not you."

He took a step backward and rather than prolong the experience I drew the knife across my forearm and the watery, orange venom that flowed through my veins came out. The new guy stared at my arm in a trance.

"See? It's obviously not blood." I pointed at Skeeter, "I could do it to him too just to prove this isn't a trick."

Skeeter snorted, "Like hell you will. I'm not letting you cut me. Cut him. Then he'll know it isn't a trick."

I asked the new guy, "Do you want me to? That would prove it." I turned the knife towards him, "You could do it yourself."

He shook his head and placed his hand over his heart, "I have a heartbeat."

"Yes, you have a heartbeat. But that's not blood pumping through it. It's venom."

He said, "Give me the knife."

"Don't give him the knife!" Skeeter exclaimed. "Give him a needle."

"I don't have a needle." I said. "Do you have a needle?"

The new guy said, "I just want to check. Give me the knife."

"OK, but don't cut your arm off, they don't grow back." I offered him the knife but then pulled it back quickly, "And don't go too deep... you can still bleed to death. Uh, venom to death I mean." I extended the knife to him again.

He took it and quickly drew it across the pad of his thumb, wincing from the pain but staring mesmerized at the venom that trickled out from the wound. After about thirty seconds Skeeter took a step closer and said in a soft voice, "We aren't fucking with you, man."

The new guy said, "You don't look like vampires."

Skeeter has always been self conscious about his looks. Being a scrawny vampire with a crooked nose tends to make him a tad defensive when it comes to the notion that all vampires are good looking hunks or sexy babes. He gave him a dirty look, "What's that supposed to mean?"

He ignored Skeeter and asked, "And I'm a vampire too?"

I said, "Yes, but before you freak out..."

He looked over to the mirror that hung by the entrance, "I look exactly the same."

Skeeter snorted, "There you go, you don't look like a vampire either." As the new guy went over to the mirror to investigate further Skeeter added, "When you become a vampire your appearance doesn't change. Did you think that once you're bitten some mystical plastic surgeon shows up to rearrange your bone structure or that you magically get abs of steel?"

The new guy turned away from the mirror. "And I have a reflection. I thought vampires didn't cast a reflection."

I motioned him over to the couch, "I'm sure you have a lot of questions. How about we all sit down and Skeeter and I will do our best to explain everything." As he moved toward the ratty couch I said, "By the way, this is Skeeter and I'm the Duke."

He turned to me sharply, "The Duke? You're a duke? Like the...uh..."

Skeeter offered, "Like the duke of Earl?"

The new guy shrugged, "Sure."

"It's just a nickname." I said, sitting down in an overstuffed easy chair that faced the couch.

"I'm Albert." The new guy said.

"Nice to meet you, Albert." I settled back into the chair and crossed my legs, "So, first of all, do you have any questions?"

"About a million." He said with a frown.

I frowned too, "Yeah, I guess you would..."

He said, "For starters, where the hell am I?"

Skeeter flipped his leg over the side of the chair he was sitting in and said, "In our apartment."

"In MY apartment." I corrected.

Albert looked around, "I see. And why did you bring me here?"

Skeeter smiled, "We couldn't exactly leave you lying there un-dead in your backyard."

"And why was I un-dead in the first place?"

Skeeter and I both looked down at our laps sheepishly. "Well," I said, "We kind of got caught without supplies."

Skeeter laughed, "Road trip gone bad, man."

"Shut up, Skeeter." I said, "Look, I'm really sorry about this. We screwed up. We were short on blood, we got lost, our car ran out of gas and… well, the fever hit."

"The fever?"

"If you go more than two days without blood, you get kind of antsy."

Skeeter nodded, "Like heroin withdrawal, blood lust kind of antsy."

Albert narrowed his eyes but said nothing.

"It wasn't even you we were after." I said, "It was your chickens."

Albert's face contorted into a look of disgust, "You were trying to suck the blood out of my chickens?"

"And then you kind of surprised us." Skeeter said.

Albert looked off into space, obviously trying to remember. "So you attacked me and sucked my blood?"

Skeeter nodded, "In a nutshell."

"So now I'm dead?"

"Un-dead." Skeeter said.

"A vampire?"

"Just like us!" Skeeter said proudly.

Albert looked us over again, "I don't feel any different. My wrist still hurts from when I sprained it a couple days ago."

Skeeter said, "That will all be better soon."

Albert rotated his wrist a few times, "So I'm immortal? I can't get hurt anymore? I'll live forever?"

Skeeter frowned, "I meant, well, sprains heal in time."

I cleared my throat, "Yes, you're immortal, but not like... immortal, immortal."

Albert narrowed his eyes at me, "Can you explain that?"

"Well, it's like this: You don't age, you don't get sick, but if you get hit by a bus or something, then you're pretty much dead. You're immortal, but not invincible."

"I thought that vampires could only get killed by a stake to the heart or by going out into sunlight or..."

I shook my head, "A vampire can get killed just like any human. We just don't age or get sick."

"Except for the blood lust sickness thing." Skeeter ventured.

"Yeah, except for the blood thing..."

"But you can go out in the sun, so that's a good thing." Skeeter said with a smile.

Albert ignored him, "Do you eat?"

"No," I said. "We can't eat. Well, we can... but we can't digest it."

Skeeter said, "We can drink though."

"But we can't digest that either." I said.

Skeeter smiled, "But nothing beats that morning cup of coffee."

I nodded, "Things like caffeine, sugar and alcohol still affect us physiologically."

Skeeter took a cigarette out of a crumpled pack and lit one, "Nicotine!" He said, saluting Albert with the cigarette.

"Vampires can smoke?"

"Sure," Skeeter said, "We smoke. Dude, if you can't eat, you're going to have to do something. Show me a vampire and I'll show you someone with an oral fixation. Cigarettes, gum, toothpicks, nail biters..."

"It's true." I said, lighting a cigarette of my own, "You never realize how much you miss food, even if you're not hungry."

Skeeter said, "Vampirism is also 420 friendly." He leaned forward toward Albert, "Speaking of which, I don't suppose you're carrying are you?"

Albert ignored him and looked at me with a pained expression, "Are you guys fucking with me?"

We shook our heads.

"Do you guys sleep in coffins?"

I laughed, "No, in beds."

Albert's brow creased as he looked at Skeeter and I. His eyes seemed to take in our appearance again. Me in my jeans and t-shirt, Skeeter in his skater shorts and flannel shirt. "You guys just don't look like vampires. This has to be bullshit."

Skeeter was obviously pissed off, "Yeah, we don't look like vampires! We don't wear leather pants and designer shirts! Do you know how much that shit costs? And besides, people who dress like that look like fucking idiots."

Just then the door to my apartment opened and Cherry walked in. This was a good thing because not only is Cherry a vampire, but she looks like one too. That is to say, she looks like a vampire because she's Goth, as many new vampires tend to be. She was pale as death, with jet black hair cut in a bob, with way too much eye liner and of course the black clothes and overdone silver jewelry. To be fair, she wasn't completely Goth, she just looked like it. Cherry was a bit of a flake, kind of a cross between a hippy and a Goth. She was a gippy, but a good friend nonetheless. Skeeter was madly in love with her, but there were some obvious physical limitations to overcome. This isn't the time to get into it, but male vampires are impotent. I didn't have the heart to explain this to

Albert because whether you're human or otherwise, impotency is not something you want to talk about with a new acquaintance.

Cherry cast a deprecating eye at Albert, sitting there looking very rural in his overalls. "Who's the hayseed?"

Skeeter said, "A newbie."

That changed everything. Cherry glided into the living room, sitting down on the couch next to Albert and in her vampy whisper she said, "How are you adjusting?"

Albert just stared at her.

She turned to me, "Have you explained everything to him yet?"

I shook my head, "We just got started but…"

"Oh good!" She said with a bright smile. She turned back to Albert, "My name is Cherry. I was re-born 3 years ago." Re-born, oh brother. Cherry says stuff like that all the time. She loves being a vampire. After she was turned it took me 6 months to get her to stop pronouncing it "vamp-ear".

She turned back to me, "Have you given your testimony yet?"

"No. But that's not really important…"

She turned back to Albert, "The Duke is our sire, Skeeter's and mine. He created us."

I hate that fucking term, "sire." It sounds so lame and creepy. And I didn't create them, I bit them.

"The Duke has been a vampire since 1978."

Skeeter laughed, "That's why he loves KC and the Sunshine Band!"

Cherry continued, "And Skeeter looks like a Kurt Cobain wanna-be because he was turned in 1992."

Skeeter gave her a hurt look.

She said, "The Duke was 25, Skeeter was 21 and I was 19. But vampirism doesn't discriminate against age. There are older vampires…"

That's true. If someone gets turned into a vampire when they're 67 years old, poof: you got a 67 year old vampire, complete with grey hair, wrinkles and age spots. Vampire venom isn't drawn from the fountain of youth. You don't revert back in time to when you were young, you stay the same age. I like how in the movies you can have these kids who are vampires who never grow up but you never see any senior citizen vampires going around in their cardigan sweaters and nipple high corduroy pants. Believe me, they're out there and they're just as grumpy and depressing as their human counterparts.

"… but they tend to keep to themselves." She didn't mention that most of them commit suicide because life in perpetuity may be tolerable when you're in your twenties but is probably agony to someone past retirement age.

Albert looked at Cherry and asked, "So, does this mean that there are other things out there? Like werewolves or ghosts or…"

She nodded solemnly. "There are many otherworldly creatures that walk among us. There are sprites and spirits and…"

Albert looked at Skeeter and me for confirmation. We shook our heads.

Albert blurted out, "Do we have super strength?"

Cherry looked at him with a disgusted expression, "No."

He looked disappointed, "Any special powers?"

She brightened again, "Being one of the chosen means that you have heightened perception, a communion with the ebb and flow of the universe, a greater sense of life. Your five senses are charged with acute awareness and understanding."

Albert looked at Skeeter and me again. We shook our heads.

Cherry continued, "Being a vampire is to walk in concert with all living things and…"

Albert sighed, "So no super powers huh?"

She scowled, "Did you think that vampires have fucking x-ray vision? We're not a bunch of spandex wearing superheroes you stupid hick."

He said, "I'm sorry, I didn't mean to imply that being a vampire isn't cool."

She snorted, "Damn right it's cool. A lot cooler than being a farmer."

He turned back to me, "So what do I do now?"

I asked, "Are you married?"

He shook his head.

"Close family?"

He shook his head again and this caused Cherry to turn to me with a smug look. She has a theory that there are only certain kinds of people who get turned into vampires once they've been bitten. Certainly the survival rate is very, very low. I would estimate that only one in a thousand victims become vampires once infected with venom. Of course that's only a ballpark estimation, math and statistics were never my strong suit but the fact remains that most people die right away from blood loss (as you can imagine.)

I know you might be thinking that we're a bunch of mass murderers, but we're not. My friends and I almost never bite anyone. We get our blood from other, more humane sources. If we can't get human blood (which is the preference) then we settle for animal blood. It isn't as potent but you can live indefinitely on it. That was the reason why Skeeter and I were in the country to begin with. We were supposed to be meeting a cattle farmer who was going to supply us with a steady stream of cow blood. The fact that we got lost, ran out of gas and ended up walking 10 miles in a hail storm and were forced to attack Albert when all we wanted was his chickens is besides the point. The thing is, we don't attack people and when we do "attack" it's usually with a syringe... but I won't bother getting in to that now.

Anyway, Cherry's theory is that the only ones who turn into vampires are those who are destined for it. They have no family, few friends, and can basically disappear from their former lives without causing a fuss. She thinks vampirism is caused by divine intervention. My own opinion is that it's based on certain genetic coding that lends itself to vampirism. But of course that's just my way of saying that I don't have a clue.

I replied to Albert, "You can do what you want. You can go back to the farm. You raise chickens so you have a steady food supply."

"Chicken blood." He said in a dry voice.

"It's not so bad," I said with a smile. "It tastes like chicken."

He slumped down on the couch, "This has to be a dream."

I went over and put my hand on his shoulder, "It's not so bad. I mean, you get to live forever."

Skeeter laughed, "Unless you get into an unfortunate combine accident."

I glared at Skeeter and then said to Albert, "Just make sure you keep topped up. With blood I mean. You only go berserk unless you run out."

"How much do I need to drink?"

Cherry said, "If you can get human blood, you only need half a pint every few days. For animal blood, a pint a day to be safe." She patted his leg, "Stick with the chickens Homer, you don't seem cut out to be a night stalker."

He looked up at me, "Can I go home now?"

I smiled, "Sure. We had to borrow your truck. It's parked downstairs."

He stood up, looked at Skeeter and then to Cherry and mumbled, "It was nice meeting you."

Cherry picked up the game controller and Skeeter came around the table to sit next to her, "See ya, Albert. And hey man..." Albert looked at him expectantly. Skeeter gave him a sheepish smile, "Sorry about killing you."

Albert looked like he was about to say something but just nodded. "See you."

Albert and I went down the stairs that led to my coffee shop and went through the store room, around the counter and weaved our way through the tables to the exit. Once outside, we paused on the sidewalk and squinted at the setting sun. It was a pleasant summer evening and it still smelled nice because of the recent rain. He turned to the building and looked at the faded letters on the glass window, "Phang's?"

I chuckled, "It used to be Phang's Grocery. The owner was Malaysian. I bought the store a couple years ago and turned it into a coffee shop. Now it's Phang's Coffee." I raised my hand, "And yeah, it's a lame joke but I thought the name was fitting."

I handed him the keys to his truck and said, "Just stay on this street until you get to Third, then take a left and that'll take you to the highway."

He glanced up at the street sign that read "Knecks Street." He raised an eyebrow, "Phang's on Knecks?"

I smiled, "Funny, right?"

He opened the door to the truck and got inside. "If you say so."

He rolled the window down and I leaned closer. "Listen Albert, I would say I'm sorry too, but it's not a bad life. Not really. Not when you compare it to the alternative of growing old and dying."

He nodded, "I guess so."

I fished in my pocket and handed him my card. "If you have any questions or just want to talk... my email is on there too."

He took the card. "Thanks."

I watched him drive off and then turned back to the store. It was going to be a busy day tomorrow.

Episode Two

"The Gang"

The worst thing about running a coffee shop that is frequented by vampires is that the place is always crawling with vampires.

Most of them have jobs but when they aren't working, they're hanging around my place. I suppose when you have an infinite amount of time to kill, you get bored. Plus, when you need blood to survive, you're always on the lookout for a fix and it's comforting to stay near a place that usually has a steady supply.

Phang's is the place to be if you need blood. I charge a moderate fee even though I feel compelled to look after them, since I was the one that turned them all into vampires. Cherry thinks that I have a gift, that somehow my venom is specially designed for "siring" these monsters. I just think it's a fluke.

Before you get the impression that I'm some kind of vampire baby mama, out making a bunch of newbies for kicks and welfare checks, I'm not. It doesn't happen often. Over the last twenty five years, I've been responsible for changing seven people. That really isn't that bad when you think about it. I mean, that's over a whole quarter century of being a blood sucking fiend.

Of the seven vampires, four of them still hang around regularly. Albert, who you just met, was the seventh. The remaining two didn't last long. But I'd rather not talk about that just yet.

Aside from the weekends, where the no good vampires have nothing better to do than hang around my shop, Mondays are usually the busiest day of the week. Vampires hate Mondays too. We all need our coffee, cigarettes and some sympathetic ears to bitch to.

Phang's is a small coffee shop that I opened in 1998, during the coffee shop craze. It was busy for a couple years because it's situated in the "artsy" part of town, sandwiched in between an art gallery and a vintage clothing store. The whole block has more than its share of record stores, funky furniture outlets, pawn shops and yes, coffee shops. Knecks Street has five coffee shops, all better appointed and much more profitable than mine. If I didn't charge for blood, I would be out of business in no time.

The shop has a couch (courtesy of one of the funky furniture outlets) and two tables. It also has a long counter with stools and when my friends come in, that's generally where they perch themselves like strung out crows. The size of the shop, (and the rotten coffee) are contributing factors to the poor business, but the reality of it is that humans tend to shy away from vampires. We don't stink or anything (at least as far as I can tell) but we seem to give off a repellent because people have a natural tendency to stay away. I think that's the reason why vampires have remained a secret for as long as we have. That and the fact that we don't look like Hollywood vampires (no fangs, stylish clothes or drop dead good looks). For the most part, we're all on friendly terms with the humans around us but aside from Cherry, who has a bit of a cult following with certain creepy humans, we keep to ourselves.

Skeeter was sitting at a table, doodling on a napkin. A cup of coffee was steaming in front of him and a cigarette was burning down, ignored in an overflowing ashtray. Cherry was at the counter, telling me about a dream she had about a wood nymph or some such nonsense. The door swung open and Stan stalked to the counter.

Stan is one of mine. I turned him about five years ago and he still hasn't forgiven me. He's the most miserable creature you'd ever meet but I suppose he has a reason to be. When I turned him into a vampire, he had just inherited a ton of money from an uncle he never knew, he was (and still is) handsome, and barely into his thirties. He was dating three different men (yeah, he's gay) and basically had his whole life mapped out. He was happy. That was five years ago.

He ran his fingers over his bald head (oh yeah, that's another reason why he's pissed at me – when I bit him he had a shaved head and since our hair doesn't grow, he's been stuck with the same "look" for half a decade.) "Give me a coffee."

"Hey Chuckles, how was your weekend?" I asked.

He slumped down into a stool. "Don't call me that. Just give me a coffee."

"Bad weekend?"

"They're all bad."

Cherry piped up from two stools away. "Hey Chuckles, if you ever want to borrow one of my wigs, just let me know."

Stan grumbled, "Fuck off vampire bitch." He looked back to me, "Give me a coffee!"

"Give me two dollars!" I yelled back.

I poured him the coffee and placed it in front of him and he threw a crumpled fiver on the counter. "Fucking Mondays."

For the next half hour we all kept to ourselves, splitting up the morning paper and reading sections. A customer came in and went up to the counter to order a large low fat half and half cappuccino and my response was to stare at him wordlessly. Cherry stood up, "I'll make it." She went around the counter and started working the dials on the coffee machines that were a mystery to me.

While he waited, the stranger at the counter made little flirting glances to Stan who was obliviously reading the paper. The door opened again and the Prof came in. The Prof was a teacher (and vampire) who graded high school correspondence papers from his home. He was almost 50 years old and looked 70. He'd had a hard life. He only came to the coffee shop for blood or to talk to me about his theories on vampirism. If he could help it, he never spoke to anyone else there. I suppose I was the exception because I was the one who had turned him, back in 1987.

He went up to the bar and put a brown paper bag on the counter. "Duke, a cup of the finest human blood if you please." I let out a nervous laugh and motioned to the human customer with a tilt of my head. He corrected himself by saying, "Coffee of course."

I didn't have a chance to get a cup of either before he loudly proclaimed, "Duke, I believe I've figured out a solution to our erectile dysfunction!"

The customer looked from me to the Prof with a quizzical expression.

Then the Prof reached into the bag with a flourish and plunked down a penile pump with "Big Jack's Dong Expander" emblazoned on the side of the packaging along with a very descriptive picture of who I presumed to be Big Jack.

Cherry handed the customer his coffee and took his money. He lost no time in getting out the door. I handed the Prof his cup of blood while he was tearing the packaging off the device he had brought. He set it aside, took a delicate sip of his blood and licked his lips, "Ah, a good vintage." After another little sip he said, "You know my theory on erections, Duke."

I nodded politely, though I really did not want to have this conversation in front of Cherry, the guys or Big Jack.

"Our bodies are now in a state of preservation." The Prof said.

Stan let out a gruff laugh, "Yeah, we have formaldehyde in our veins. We're like frogs in a biology class."

The Prof ignored him, which is what he always did. "I've often theorized that if one went through the metamorphosis while they were physically aroused, that state would then carry over into their new form."

Skeeter came over to the counter and sat down next to Stan. His eyes went back and forth from the penis enlarger to Cherry, who was listening to the Prof with amusement clearly etched on her face. Cherry giggled, "A vampire walking around with a permanent boner."

The Prof went on as if she hadn't spoken. "We know that our neurological receptors still function, otherwise we wouldn't react to things like alcohol or caffeine. The same is true for our emotions; we can be happy, sad, angry..."

"Horny." Cherry offered with another giggle.

"So our hormones are still intact, but without the physical manifestations that would normally occur."

"Hard ons." Cherry said.

"But we also know that our bodies still react to things like pain and pleasure. Somewhere there is a disconnect. We can't alter our physical forms..."

Stan said in a sad voice, "If I'd known I would be in this body for eternity, I would have done more sit ups."

Cherry said, "Why do you even care about boners? You're like 80 years old."

The Prof scowled at her, "I am... was, 49 years old and for your information, prior to my transformation, I was a bit of a tom cat."

Cherry laughed, "So you've discovered Big Jack to solve the limp noodle problem."

He turned back to me, "If aided by certain medications, a temporary alteration may be possible."

Skeeter asked in an eager tone, "Does it work?"

The Prof let out an exasperated sigh, finally deigning to acknowledge someone else's presence. "Did you fail to notice that I brought the device in its original packaging? I obviously haven't experimented yet."

I think Skeeter would have volunteered right then but there was another interruption in the form of Gem, a nurse who worked at St. Peter's hospital downtown. She was my blood dealer, my plasma pusher, my connection with the lurid world of underground trafficking in human go juice. She was a horrible person. A greedy bitch. A rude, malevolent and unethical c-word.

She came right up to the counter and shoved her way in between Skeeter and Stan. "Duck, we need to talk." She liked calling me "Duck."

She looked at Big Jack's product, and then smirked at Cherry, "Getting ready to take on the whole team?"

Cherry gave her a sweet smile, "Can I get you anything Gem? Coffee, donut, fork to the eyeball?"

Gem let out a snorting kind of dismissive laugh and then snapped her fingers at me, "C'mon duck, we have business to discuss."

I sighed, "Cherry, can you watch the shop for me?"

She saluted me, "No problem little buddy."

Gem walked around the counter like she owned the place and made a bee line straight for my office in the back. She sat down on top of the desk and crossed her legs. She had nice legs. In fact she had a lot of nice everything; everything except personality and a functioning soul.

"We have to renegotiate." She said, looking down at her nails.

I leaned against the door. "Why? Is there a shortage of human blood nowadays?"

"There will be for you if you don't cough up."

"How much more?" I reluctantly asked.

"Double."

"Fuck off, Gem."

She smiled, "Gladly. But if I fuck off, so does your readily available product. You'll have to go back to sucking off hobos, but you probably did that before you became a vampire."

"I'm not paying double."

"Then I guess you're going thirsty."

"I could go 25 percent more."

"You can go double or you can fuck yourself."

I stared at her, trying to fathom how I ended up in business with someone like her. She kept smiling at me. I shook my head, "I can't afford to pay double."

She pointed to the wall, "You can charge those leeches double, then you'll make out just fine."

"THEY can't afford double either."

"Then I guess THEY can go thirsty too."

"Or I could just report you." I said in a snarl.

She laughed, "Absolutely, because I'm sure you wouldn't mind bringing you and your troop into the limelight. I think secrecy is still

pretty   high   on   your   list."
"I could make an anonymous phone call."

Her smile vanished as she stood up and walked over to me. "Little Duckie, if anything happens to me then I'm the one that will start making some anonymous phone calls. I'm pretty sure that murder is still a punishable crime. Especially an open and shut case with plenty of photographic evidence." She smiled again, "Look, our arrangement benefits me too. The hospital keeps a much sharper eye on the narcotics, so blood is a less risky commodity. I appreciate your business and since you're such a valuable customer, it's in my best interest to keep your supplied." She looked at me with a seductive smirk, "I would consider a discount," she licked her lips, "If you changed your mind on my offer."

Her offer was to supply blood on the cheap if I changed her into a vampire. The thought of her being alive for eternity was way too repulsive.

"Not a chance."

"Have it your way." She patted me on the cheek as she walked by, "Double. Let me know by Thursday."

I let out a long sigh, remaining in the doorway to the office. Gem had me by the balls and we both knew it. I'd been trying to find an alternative source for the last year but striking deals for blood wasn't the easiest of transactions to make. I let out another sigh and headed back to the counter.

Gem was gone, a couple customers were being served by Cherry and the Prof, Stan and Skeeter had gone over to a table to continue their discussion in muted tones. When the humans were gone I leaned forward against the counter and said, "Gem wants double."

Cherry hissed, "That bitch. Please let me kill her."

I shook my head, "We need her."

"We need blood." Cherry said, "Not her." She slammed her hand down on the counter, "Let me gut her. She's a healthy girl; she's got enough blood in her to keep us going for a few days."

I gave her a disapproving glare, "We don't kill people. You know that."

"Then let me wound her! Please boss."

Stan came over to the counter. "This is bullshit. We can't afford to pay double. I have some money, but not enough to pay that much, not for long anyway."

"I could sell another painting." Cherry ventured.

"I can pick up another shift at the warehouse." Skeeter said.

I said, "Yeah, but how long will that carry us? Especially if one of us needs to feast."

Feasting. This is a weird fever that every vampire goes through once every few years. What happens is normal amounts of blood just don't cut it. It's like the regular doses don't get absorbed into the system and you have to drink and drink (and drink some more) until you're completely bloated. It takes about a gallon of blood to cure you and after a solid day of sleep, you're back to normal.

I said, "We need to find an alternative supply, at least for the next little while. If we can squeeze her pocketbook a bit and make her wait for us, she'll have to drop the price. Supply is worthless without demand."

"We could have another blood drive!" Cherry said hopefully.

A few months back we had the brilliant idea of holding a community blood drive. We put up posters and I bought the equipment (the donor couch was still in the storeroom) and we had Cherry and Skeeter dress up in nurse's uniforms. Skeeter (who was a maestro with a needle and a blood bag) showed her how to draw blood and we had about a dozen people show up to donate.

The problem was that Cherry had been living off animal blood since her "re-birth" and underestimated her will power when it came to being around human blood. Skeeter was working on the first donor and when Cherry caught a whiff of the blood, she lost it. She latched onto the woman's arm and started sucking like a newborn (a literal newborn). The woman understandably freaked out but Cherry wouldn't let go. She held on and kept right on sucking. The woman bashed her over the head with her purse and although that wouldn't be enough to stop someone in the throes of a blood lust frenzy, Cherry had sucked up a few ounces and that was enough to make her pass out. She fell back, her uniform covered in blood and spit, the donor was screaming and bolted for the door. Thankfully the coffee shop is so small, we could only bring in a couple people at a time and the other donor was quickly ushered away by Stan and Skeeter before he saw anything. The other woman made a huge scene when she got out the door, screaming about vampires and blood suckers and freaks.

Even if they hadn't all taken off in a panic, we couldn't have brought in any more people, what with the blood that was splattered across the donor's chair and Cherry laying on her back with a satisfied smile on her face and blood dripping down her chin. I wasn't invited to any more community meetings after that.

"No blood drives." I said.

We were all quietly contemplating our options for a few minutes and then Cherry said, "I could tell Tabitha and Chagrin the truth about me and have them be our donors."

"No." I said. "We will not be telling them anything."

I didn't care for Cherry's friends because, well, they were annoying. They would have hung around her (and by extension, the coffee shop) 24 hours a day if I allowed it. Tabitha and Chagrin were vampire worshippers and they thought that Cherry was just like them, obsessed with vampire culture. Fortunately for Cherry (and for me) she wasn't nearly as annoying as her black clad friends.

"But why not?" She said in a pouty voice. "Then we would never have to worry about running out of blood. They wouldn't say anything."

Stan said, "Those tittering twats can't be trusted."

"Just because none of you losers have any friends doesn't give you the right to disrespect mine."

"You can't tell them Cherry." I said in my authoritative, fatherly voice.

She sat there pouting for a few seconds and then said, "This blows."

I said, "Skeeter and I will just go prowling for a few weeks."

When Skeeter and I went out, we would find some drunks and make an involuntary withdrawal. If we could find someone all on their own and passed out, we could siphon off some of their blood without them ever knowing it happened. We were always careful about not taking too much. It was a bit labor intensive because it involved cruising different bars and waiting for a drunk to separate themselves from the pack, so to speak.

"Or we could throw a party!" Cherry said with a beaming smile. "Then we would have them all in one place. We get them totally shit faced and as they pass out, we get them to another room and drain the fuckers dry!" She checked herself, "OK, not dry. But we take our fair share. If we can get ten or fifteen people here, that would hold us for a month! We already have all the stuff from the blood drive."

I smiled, "That's actually a pretty good idea."

Episode Three

"We're All Party People"

"Jesus, Cherry, how many people did you invite?" I asked in a harsh tone as I surveyed the seventy or so people crammed into the coffee house.

She shrugged, "Maybe four or five people at the most. You know how these things happen." Someone knocked over the coat stand near the door and I scowled at the perpetrator. Cherry took a drag from her cigarette and said, "You should be more concerned about Skeeter. He's got at least 3 people laid out in the back."

"He's got what?" I blurted.

She shrugged again.

I squeezed myself through the crowd of people that were milling around the bar and made my way into the back room. There were four people on the floor, all hooked up to their own I.V. Skeeter was bent over a guy, adjusting the needle.

I had to stop myself from shouting, "Skeeter, what the hell?" I went over to him and hissed, "One at a time only! What if one of them wakes up and sees you siphoning off their buddies?"

He said, "No need to worry... Cherry and I came up with a good plan."

"Oh no."

"We figured out a way to stream line the process. It would have been way too difficult to try to pick them off one at a time."

I felt my eyes narrow. "What did you do?"

He smiled, "Flunitrazepam."

"You roofied them?"

"Just a half dose!"

"I'm going to kill you... what are we going to do with seventy passed out people?"

Cherry came into the room, "Keep your voices down! They can hear you out there!"

Skeeter said, "And we didn't roofie everyone... just about a dozen or so."

Cherry glared at Skeeter and gave her head a quick shake.

Skeeter frowned, "More than a dozen?"

She shrugged.

"So." I said, "The question remains, what are we going to do with seventy passed out people?"

Cherry shrugged, "Drain a couple pints from each of them. Let them sleep it off and send them on their way in the morning."

Suddenly, we heard a loud crash coming from the coffee shop and all three of us made for the door to see what had happened. We stopped dead in our tracks when we saw that everyone in the shop had collapsed. Bodies were slumped over tables, sprawled back in chairs but most of the people were on the floor.

I turned to Skeeter, "You said you guys only gave them half a dose!"

Skeeter looked to Cherry for help and she shrugged, "What do I look like, a pharmacist? How the hell do I know what half a dose is?"

Tabitha, one of Cherry's friends, came out of the bathroom, wobbled over to the counter and sat down heavily on the stool. She looked at us with bleary eyes and said, "I think... there's something wrong with the punch." Then she gently laid her head down on the bar and closed her eyes.

"Skeeter." I said.

"Yeah?"

"Get the syringes."

Skeeter worked the room at lightning speed. Swab, poke, suck, remove, swab again. The coffee shop looked like the triage from M.A.S.H. I lifted one girl's arm and felt its dead weight. Cherry was across the room unhooking a bag filled with blood. I called out to her, "How long will they be out for?"

She stood up straight and scowled, "Again... not a pharmacist."

I scowled back, "But speaking as a chick that's probably been roofied before?"

She returned her attention to the bag and muttered, "Not a nice thing to say, Boss."

"Sorry." I said and went over to help Skeeter drag one of the people up to a sitting position.

Skeeter said, "I wonder if we'll all pass out after drinking this blood."

"I don't think so." I said, "Even when we drink from the drunks, it barely affects us."

"Still," He said, "I bet it'll be a mellow vintage."

We were over halfway through the crowd and we had almost filled the big chest freezer in the backroom. Once it was at capacity, we would be using the fridge and the upright cooler. Despite my previous (and ongoing) misgivings, we would be well stocked for the coming months.

Skeeter inserted the needle into a big teenaged guy and said, "How come Stan and The Prof aren't here helping?"

I said, "Because they're paying customers. You and Cherry aren't."

Cherry said, "That's not fair... just because..." Her eyes suddenly went wide and she pointed to the guy that Skeeter was busy draining. "He's waking up! Quick, clonk him on the head!"

Skeeter looked around wildly for a second or two and then stopped, "Wait, did you say 'clonk'?"

Cherry yelled, "Just do something!"

Skeeter's head swiveled around, searching for something clonk worthy and decided on a chair. The guy on the floor let out a groan and I quickly went over to him and knelt down, putting my hand on his forehead, "Just go back to sleep." I said in a soothing voice. He immediately closed his eyes again.

Skeeter was dumbfounded, "How did you do that?"

Cherry had come over as well. "Yeah, where the hell did that come from?"

I shook my head, "I have no idea."

I didn't give it much thought as the memory itself seemed to be fading as I quickly went around helping Skeeter and Cherry collect the blood and arrange the bodies...er...people, in a more natural position. It took us almost two hours to finish up and we were exhausted. Skeeter and Cherry were sitting at a table, sharing a cup of well-earned blood and I was behind the counter, smoking a cigarette. I rubbed my hand down my face and then the front door opened.

"Shit," I muttered; we had forgotten to lock the door… but since most people avoided Phang's, it was a forgivable mistake. I looked at the clock on the wall and saw that it was 3 in the morning so the alarm bells started to go off in my head. They had a good reason to be too, because the person who walked in was Gem.

She strode toward me, seemingly oblivious to all the bodies…er…people, on the floor. She said, "I heard you were throwing a party."

I said, "Your invitation must have been lost in the mail."

She finally turned around to survey the scene around us. "I might have figured. Are they dead?"

I was disgusted by her casual tone. "No, they're just asleep."

As if to confirm what I had said, she went over to one of the bodies…er… whatever, you know what I mean, and checked their pulse. She straightened back up, "So you figured you could just tap into your own supply?"

"Well, yeah, that was the plan."

She reached into her purse and took out her cell phone. She smirked, "I wonder what it would take for me not to call the police."

Without even realizing what I was doing, my hand struck out and grasped her wrist and slammed her hand down on top of the counter. I felt my lips curl in a snarl and heard my voice come out as a growl, "I wonder what it would take for me not to kill you right now."

Her eyes registered shock and, I'm ashamed to admit how much it delighted me, fear. Both Skeeter and Cherry were on their feet, staring at me.

Gem's voice actually trembled, "I have evidence... I have pictures..." She tried to pull her hand away but my grip was like a vice. I looked down at my hand like I was having an out of body experience. "Let go, you're hurting me."

I released her wrist and saw the white pressure marks from my hand. I looked back at her face and I saw that she was struggling to regain her composure. She massaged her wrist with her other hand and said, "That's better. You know you can't hurt me."

"Do I?" I snarled, once again surprising myself.

"I saw you kill those men. I TAPED you killing them! If anything happens to me, that tape goes right to the cops."

I sighed, back to my old self. "You don't need to remind me of that every time we see each other."

She smirked, "Apparently I do because every time we see each other, you try to weasel out of our deal."

"So now our deal includes blackmail."

She laughed, "Our deal has always included blackmail."

"I meant over this..." I swept my arm around the room to indicate the supine forms all around us.

"Just one more nail in the coffin... if you'll pardon the term. By the way, DO you sleep in a coffin?"

I sighed, "You're the cause of this, Gem. If you hadn't gotten so fucking greedy, we would have never had to do this."

She smiled, "Funny, I don't feel the least bit responsible. So here's what we're going to do. You're going to pay me double our monthly fee. For, let's say six months." She glanced around the room. "I would say that's how much blood you harvested tonight. Then, in six months, our deliveries will resume at the same price."

"So what you're saying is, I'll pay you double... for no product at all... and then, when we're dried up, then you'll start sending the blood again... at double the price."

Her smile easily transformed into her smirk. "Correct."

Cherry spoke up, "I say we kill her."

Skeeter said, "That's my vote too."

Gem turned around to face them but she didn't say a word because the front door opened again. I muttered, "I really have to remember to lock that thing."

I couldn't make out who was at the door but I could tell that it was a woman. As she entered, all of us stood stock still as she glided into the room. She was tall, with a graceful figure and long black hair that seemed to shimmer in the dim light. She was without a doubt the most beautiful woman I had ever seen. She was dressed in a long black coat that came to her knees and her calves were covered in sheer stockings. Without any thought of what I was doing, I moved around the counter to meet her. Her luminescent green eyes were zeroed in on me and me alone. Without a pause she reached up her hands and cupped my face, and then she kissed me. Her lips were cool but soft and moist and tasted like... sweet blood. Her voice was rich, melodic and she had a British accent. She whispered against my lips, "My son..."

Gem muttered, "Now THAT'S a vampire."

Episode Four

"Lame and Creepy"

She stroked my cheek and I felt my skin tingle as her long nails caressed me, "I've been searching for you for so long."

Her eyes were unblinking, hypnotic and I gulped, "Nice to meet you."

I heard Gem's voice, "I don't know who you are but…"

Without taking her eyes off me, the woman raised her hand and said, "Silence. You will leave now."

I watched with incredulity as Gem picked her purse off the counter and walked stiffly toward the door. The woman turned my face back to hers with her index finger, "Come my son, we must talk."

She walked through the door to the backroom and without so much as a glance at Skeeter or Cherry, I followed her inside. She began to walk to the office and then noticed the four people still asleep on the floor. She snapped her fingers and four pairs of eyes immediately opened. Her voice was commanding and not to be disobeyed. "Get out. Rouse your companions in the other room and take them with you. Now." The four people stood up with blank expressions and marched out the door in single file. The woman turned to me, "Have no concerns. They will not remember this night."

I cleared my throat again, "Oh, well… that's good."

She continued to the office and I followed like a puppy, entranced and enraptured by her. As soon as I crossed the threshold of the doorway she turned around quickly and embraced me. Her kiss was longer, deeper and more passionate. I saw stars and for the first time a few decades, I could feel my body responding. She broke the kiss off and whispered, "My darling, I'm so sorry. I should have never left you but I was pursued and had to flee. I tried to find you but they kept stopping me, blocking me every step of the way. But they have been dealt with and nothing can stop us from being together forever." She took a quick step back and held her right thumb to her left wrist. The nail seemed to grow half an inch and it was pointed like a dagger. She drew it swiftly across the veins on her wrist. The entire room smelled something like strawberries. She held her wrist out to me and said, "Quickly now, we've waited years for your transformation. Drink!"

At that moment, there was nothing I wanted more than to sink my teeth into her flesh and despite the upsetting sight of her pale wrist dripping venom; I knew that once I tasted it, I would never want anything else again. Nevertheless, something deep inside me warned me step back, to wait, to consider... I moved away a foot or so and the aroma of her venom lessened a tiny bit. "Um, hold on a sec... Miss."

She laughed, and it was the most musical sound I'd ever heard. "How foolish of me! Of course you don't remember me at all do you?" She took an embroidered handkerchief from her coat pocket and passed it over her wrist. The wound was sealed and the smell of her venom was gone. She smiled, "Call me Persephone."

Of course she would have a name like Persephone. It couldn't be Jane or Betty.

She put her hand to my cheek and the feel of her skin on my own sent my nether regions into overdrive. Persephone was definitely a better remedy that The Prof and Big Jack. "Oh Joseph," she cooed. Joseph. That used to be my name. I hadn't used it in...

"It's been almost 40 years." She said. "I can't imagine the hell you've been living."

"Well," I sputtered, "It hasn't been ALL bad... I mean, there's the coffee shop and..."

She made a tut tut sound and pressed her index finger against my lips, "My child, you've been so brave to have survived this long in your state."

"My state? You mean...being a vampire?"

She laughed, "Sweetest heart, you aren't a vampire. Not yet. Not until you've tasted your creator's blood will you change into a vampire."

My face must have registered the shock that I felt and her laughter died. "Forgive me child! It is callous of me to laugh! I cannot imagine you existing in this state for this long. Not human, not vampire... condemned to purgatory until I could find you. Enough talk, come drink!" She moved her thumb to her wrist again and I reached out and placed my hand on hers, "Wait just a sec, OK? I have to process. You're saying I'm not a vampire?"

She sighed. "This would all be clear to you if you just drank, but if you need me to explain I will."

She turned around and went over to the desk. She swept the pile of last month's bills onto the floor and half sat/half leaned against the desk. "You have been in a state of transit since I created you. In order to become a full vampire, the survivor must drink from the creator. Then the transformation is complete. If you do not drink, you remain half human. You may walk in the daylight but your human cravings – to eat and to drink and all the fleshly desires are still present but they cannot be consumed or consummated. You are still as weak as a human, with all their frailties but you are also immortal and yet you cannot survive without blood."

I asked, "So a vampire can't be out in the sun or eat or drink..."

Her eyes flashed, "You speak of weaknesses! You compare a vampire to a human when the two are incomparable! It is like an ant to a lion… a speck of dust to a galaxy!" Her look and her tone softened, "It is like comparing a human to a God."

I said, "Tonight I was able to do things I haven't done before. I commanded someone to sleep and when Gem threatened me, I became…"

"You became fierce." She said and her eyes shined. "You were able to do these things because I was near. That was just a taste of the power you are destined to have."

I thought about how Skeeter and Cherry would react to having that kind of power. I wondered if they would even be recognizable once they changed. I didn't even consider what I would be like. As if on cue, I heard them approach. Skeeter said, "Duke, you won't believe what just happened out there."

Cherry chimed in, "It was like the Night of the Living Dead. Everyone woke up all at once and frog marched right out the door."

Persephone let out a gasp and when I turned to her, she was staring wide eyed at Skeeter and Cherry. Both of them seemed more than uncomfortable under her gaze and stood stock still, like soldiers about to be inspected by a General.

Persephone continued to stare at them but spoke to me, "How can this be? They are bitten but not converted as well. Why did I not notice them when I entered this building? Who is their creator?"

I cleared my throat, "I am, I mean to say that I was the one that… I'm not very comfortable with the whole "creator" term."

Persephone turned her face to me so fast that I expected to hear the crack of a whip. "But that's not possible! You cannot create… you aren't fully formed."

I shrugged.

She stood up quickly and came over to me, putting both her hands on my temples and said, "Show me your memories. Let me inside your mind." She turned to Skeeter and Cherry and said in a commanding tone, "Leave us."

Neither of them moved a muscle. Cherry was about to speak and I said, "It's OK guys, just give me a minute, K?"

They both turned around and began walking away without so much as a grumble. Persephone looked back to me, her eyes wide with wonder. "This is unheard of, that they should resist me and obey you. You truly must be the creator." Her eyes bore into mine and her voice sank to a whisper, "Show me…"

I felt myself go into a kind of trance, like my mind was reduced to a DVD and she was fast forwarding through it, seeing everything that I had seen or felt over my entire life. I have no idea how long it lasted, but when she was done she seemed drained. She slumped back onto the desk and looked at me wearily.

When she spoke, it was as if she was talking to herself, "I have never seen such a thing before. A half-vampire creating his own offspring." Her eyes seemed to refocus and she said to me. "Most vampires cannot become creators. For you to be able to create is… unheard of. It is remarkable and yet," she licked her lips, "It cannot be abided." Her chin rose a tiny bit, "You did well to destroy those two children."

I wasn't at all comfortable with her referring to the two men I had killed as children. I said, "They were in a frenzy, they were going to kill people. I had to stop them."

"Whatever the reason, it was well done. You acted accordingly and yet with these others, you allowed them to live."

I felt anger rising deep in my chest. "I'm responsible for them. They're my friends. They're… my family. Killing Josh and Trevor… that was the worst thing I've ever done and even now, when I think about it, I feel like someone is shoving a knife into my heart."

She stood up straight again, "Yes, I can understand why you would feel like that, but they are an abomination. In order for you to join with me, you cannot allow them to live. A half-vampire creating more half-vampires cannot be tolerated. There are strict laws. Each new vampire must be nurtured and trained, as you must be once you transform." She paused, "When you become a God, you will leave this life behind and come with me. Your new life awaits."

"Hold on Persephone. I'm not killing my friends."

"You need not be burdened, I will do it for you."

"No way." I stood up straighter, "I won't allow you to hurt them."

I thought she would get angry but instead she smiled, "Your attachment to them is, as I said, understandable. I will not force you, indeed, I could not. The ascension must be your choice. If you claim ownership of the offspring, I cannot harm them. But Joseph, consider carefully, you could be a God. You could be with me." She reached out for my hand and held it to her breast, "We could be together and live in bliss, with a passion the world has never witnessed."

I could feel my heart beat faster and I'm sure she could hear it too. She let go of my hand and said, "I will admit that I am intrigued by your... family. It is completely new to me." She stood up and glanced at the ratty couch that was pushed up against the wall, "It is almost dawn and I would like to retire now." She stretched out on the couch on her back.

I said, "Would you like a blanket or something?" I immediately felt like a twit for offering, like she was just an old friend from out of town, coming over to crash for the night. Also, I didn't have a blanket.

She smiled and shook her head, "No my sweet, I am content."

"OK then," I said as I backed toward the door. "I'll give you some privacy."

"I will see you at dusk." She said, and then closed her eyes.

I went back to the front of the store and saw that Skeeter and Cherry were sitting at a table, smoking cigarettes. I could smell the coffee brewing and I was desperate for a cup. I poured myself a cup and the very smell of it made me think about what Persephone had said about my half-human cravings for eating and drinking and what it would be like to be free of those desires. In the meantime, the coffee smelled delicious and I took a sip before going around the counter to join Skeeter and Cherry.

"So boss, are you going to tell us about the witch-queen?"

Skeeter hissed to Cherry, "Shhh! I bet she can hear every word."

I said, "Don't worry about her guys. She's asleep."

"And when she wakes up?" Cherry asked.

"You don't have to worry about her then either." I said. "And she isn't a witch, I think she's OK."

"She doesn't look OK." Skeeter mumbled into his coffee cup.

I thought about her casual tone when she said she would kill them both for me. I shuddered, "She's fine." I said, more to myself than to them. I looked at my watch, "Skeeter, you better get going. You're on the early shift this week. And Cherry, you should go home and get some rest before we open up."

Skeeter wrinkled his brow at me. "It's Sunday."

Cherry stood up and said to Skeeter, "It's just his nice way of telling us to fuck off and leave him alone." She glanced over at me, "And possibly that he's too tired to even know what day it is. Let's go."

I gave her a weary smile, "Thanks."

As she deposited her smokes, lighter, cell phone, make up and iPod into her purse she said, "But I will expect a full report tonight. You say she's OK but she gives me the creeps... and that's saying something."

After they left I tidied up the shop, collecting all the empties and dumping ashtrays. Skeeter and Cherry had already cleared away all the evidence of our blood siphoning activities so there wasn't much for me to do expect cast about a thousand glances to the backroom and chew my fingernails.

My mind was fully occupied with undergoing the "ascension" and becoming like Persephone. I would probably have to buy a pair of leather pants and start listening to Nine Inch Nails. I didn't relish either possibility. Beyond my wild imaginings of what it would be like to be all-powerful, I always went back to the thought of my "family". Aside from Stan, the others all seemed to be perfectly content with their lot in life. Sure, The Prof was pre-occupied with erections, but other than that, we was happy to be left alone and he was a smart guy, I'm sure he could come up with something to fix our "problem". Skeeter was Skeeter, happy as long as he had a few bucks for smokes and video games and if he could spend every day with Cherry, there was nothing else he could want. As for Cherry, she loved being a vampire and given half the chance, she would go back to calling herself a "vamp-ear". She would jump at the chance that Persephone offered.

But would I? I mean, sure, who wouldn't want to be a God? Even if it was a pale, creature-of-the-night, Eye-vant-to-suck-your-blood, kind of God. It was a stupid reason, but Persephone, for all her looks, power and general aura was exactly what I hated about vampirism in general. Maybe I was acting "too cool for school", but the whole thing just seemed lame and creepy. I grabbed a rag and began to wash the tables for the third time that day.

Around six o'clock, Cherry came in and before saying hello she said, "Has the Queen of the Damned woken up yet?"

I shook my head and she sat down at the table to give me dirty looks until Skeeter showed up a few minutes later. "Has the Queen of the Damned woken up yet?"

I said, "Did you guys rehearse this?"

Skeeter smiled at Cherry, "Did you call her that too?"

Cherry ignored him and said to me, "It's almost dark, maybe you should go wake her up."

A stately voice came from behind us, causing all three of us to give a little start. "She has already awakened." I recovered as quickly as possible and thought up something just as stately to reply. "Hi. Have a good sleep?" I wanted to hide under a table.

"Thank you, yes. May we speak alone?" She didn't wait for a reply and went back through the door.

I shrugged to the guys and then threw my rag down on the counter and followed her back.

She was sitting on the couch with her legs crossed. Once again, I felt a flush of desire for her. "I have been in communication with the Council."

"There's a Council?" I asked stupidly.

"Yes." She replied with infinite patience.

"How did you communicate? Like, through your mind?"

"I used the phone."

"Ah."

After a pause she said, "They were as shocked with your situation as I was. But I have good news. They have decreed that your offspring may live."

"That's awesome!" I said, feeling a little embarrassed by my enthusiastic reply. "I mean, I wouldn't have allowed it regardless." I said, feeling even more like an idiot for adding that.

She smiled indulgently. "I am so glad to have it resolved. The Council was most understanding."

"So who is this Council? Where are they? And who are these other people you mentioned last night? You said they were blocking you from seeing me."

She said, "There will be time for all explanations. Are you ready to come away with me?"

"So how does this work? I drink from you and the others, they drink from me?"

She paused, "No, they cannot drink from you."

I bit my lip. "From you then?"

She paused and then shook her head. "Once you drink from me, you will sever the connection with them. You will not be aware of them."

"I'll just forget about them? But they need me!"

She stood up and came over to me. "My love, the ascension is a rebirth. You will lose all contact with this life."

I took a step back. "I can't do it."

Once again, I expected her to be angry but she only looked hurt and sad. She stared into my eyes and said, "We cannot be fully joined until you drink of me. The bond that we could share would be unbreakable. There is no greater connection between a vampire and their creation."

"Then you know what you're asking of me and why I have to refuse. I can't leave them."

She stared at me for a long time as if reading my mind and then she let out a sigh. "I do understand." She suddenly kissed me again and in that moment, I felt the loss, the absolute devastation, of refusing her. She broke off the kiss and said, "Perhaps in time you will reconsider."

She turned away and we both started to walk to the shop. Once through the door Skeeter and Cherry were standing there looking anxiously at us. Persephone paused and stared at Cherry. After a moment she looked back at me and said, "This girl loves that boy."

Cherry's face turned red and she began to sputter something but after a glance at Persephone, she remained silent. I thought Skeeter was about to let out a cheer.

Persephone walked to the door and blew me a kiss. "Farewell for now, my love."

I stood there feeling like a dork and waved good-bye.

Cherry gave me an expectant look, "So, are you going to tell us what that was all about?"

I smiled, "I wouldn't know where to start. How about with how you're in love with Skeeter?"

She glared at me and Skeeter's grin was enough to split his face. Before anything else could be said, the door opened and Gem walked in. Her hair wasn't done and she was dressed in sweat pants and a t-shirt. Her eyes appeared to be glazed over and her expression was blank. She walked to the counter and put down a thick legal sized envelope. Without speaking a word, she turned around marched out the door.

I opened the envelope and saw that it held two camcorder tapes and a sheaf of photographs. It was the evidence that she had been blackmailing me with and I knew that I had Persephone to thank. I was musing how cool it would be to have that kind of God-like power but my thoughts were quickly interrupted by The Prof bursting through the door. Stan was right behind him and wearing an uncharacteristic smile.

"Duke, I've got it! A proper mixture of Viagra, coupled with the penis enlarger does the trick!"

I smiled in reply and thought that I really didn't need to be a God. I already had everything I needed.

Daffodillies

It was a perfect day for the folk festival. The end of August is kind to us in Alberta; it brings sunny days with crisp mornings and cool evenings. A nice westerly breeze made sure that none of the thousand or so folk fans were uncomfortable. I spread out my blanket on the grassy hill and closed my eyes to the sun as I listened to the music.

It was an older crowd; mostly slim baby boomers with tanning bed skin that shone through brand name summer clothes. There were those in their twenties and thirties sprinkled throughout and even a younger crowd that stayed near the stage, probably waiting for the right moment to introduce a mosh pit.

I was somewhere in the middle, both in location as well as demographic. I sat in between two couples, both nearing fifty and acting a little stand offish because I look about five or so years younger than what I am. I just turned 29 but I was treated as a usurper on the folksy knoll. I was only accepted by my companions when I began to wax philosophic about Joan Baez and the Guthries. The couple on my right passed me a joint and I felt like I belonged.

After a couple hours of sitting I felt the need to stretch my legs and decided to walk down to the concession stands. I passed a few booths hawking overpriced t-shirts and coffee mugs and I bought a paper cup full of stale 7 Up.

I leaned against the side of the booth and watched a group of teenagers dance directly in front of the stage. There were four guys and maybe eight or nine girls, all in a circle, laughing and singing along as they danced night club moves to sixties tunes.

I watched them for a few minutes and then I caught myself staring at one of the girls. It wasn't a conscious thing at first. It was more like those times when your eyes get lazy and you find yourself looking at something until it goes blurry. I suppose it must have been obvious because although we were at least fifty feet away from each other, she noticed me and smiled.

It was that smile that made me snap out of it. I was no longer mindlessly looking; I was staring with a fully conscious mind. Her friends were all dressed in shorts and t-shirts but she was wearing a loose summer dress. It was pale blue with yellow designs and as she moved the dress clung, let go, clung again, and accenting her lithe body. Her hair was light blonde, medium length and so straight that it looked like she had run an iron over it. She had a pale complexion and even from so far away, I could tell that her eyes were a very light blue. When she moved to the music, my heart beat like a Gene Krupa solo.

When she did notice me, her eyes never left. She danced for me and soon after, she danced toward me. She couldn't be twenty years old. The grace of the young departs soon enough and its absence is made up for in sophistication and staid mannerisms. This girl had nothing contrived or practiced about her. When the song ended she kept dancing to me. Her eyes bored into mine, a smile mischievous and full of life. Her hips swayed as the beat continued on for her and me.

We didn't speak, even after she stopped directly in front of me. I was too rapt for words and she didn't need any. She took the cup from my hand and took a long sip before handing it back to me. She wore no makeup and the little freckles on the bridge of her nose could have been in a painting. Her neck was long and her teeth were white as dove's wings. Her eyes laughed and twinkled. Her long fingers ran through her silken hair as she leaned on one foot.

All this comes to mind now. None of that registered at the time. When she was standing in front of me all I could sense was the aura. Everything about her hit me like a strong wind; her looks, her smell, (Which was like lemon juice on rose petals - but this occurs to me only now). I was lost and finally home all at once.

"I'm Cynthia. What's your name?" I can't believe she spoke. It was too much like poetry and I stood there searching for the rhyme and meter.

"That's a nice name." I managed to stutter. "I'm Frank."

She smiled, "You don't look like a Frank. You're someone else."

"Oh?" I smiled back, "Who am I then?"

She cocked her head sideways and licked her lips as if she was thinking. "Ask me later."

Small talk belongs to the insincere. For those that destiny metes out, speaking is only an interruption. We danced to one song and I left my blanket on the hill behind. She didn't even wave to her friends as we ran hand in hand to my car.

Never doubt Destiny. It brings worlds together. It crumbles empires and creates kingdoms. It tears down and it builds up and even in this cold world where Destiny is supposed to be dead, it turns red lights green, thins traffic and carries two lovers to a tiny apartment.

Still, no words after "ask me later." The car was parked and the stairs to the third floor flew by. The door was flung open, then, once inside, it was closed and locked by her hand. My keys fell to the floor and my hand became tangled in a light blue summer dress. Her lips were on mine, and tongues that speak, curse, lecture and lie were intertwined in what is surely their true purpose.

She was on her toes, leaning against me, forcing me to stagger back and hold on to her. We fell to our knees and undressed each other. It was then that reality swirled and turned around us. After touching, tasting and mingling our moans into one song, I picked her up and carried her to the bedroom.

It would sound like a song if I could describe her touch. Her kisses would be an epic poem and all things great and wonderful would pale next to her. For all the beauty that was her, it went beyond. It was me too. I felt beautiful and sublime in her arms. It was us. A perfect union.

There was no inhibition in our nakedness. No hesitation or shame in our love making. Her hands were on my face and as we stared into each other's eyes and gasped with breathless heaves, she moaned, "Tell me, tell me." There wasn't a pause before I said that I loved her.

It wasn't a lie. It wasn't a mindless sexual edification. It was the truth. I did love her.

When the sun dipped below my window we fell apart. She lay by my side with her hand pressing against my chest. Her hair, smelling of daffodils and lilies, was dark with sweat and splayed over the pillow.

My chest rose and fell as I inhaled deeply. I turned my face and smiled, and she was smiling too. I put my hand to her cheek. "Can I ask you now?"

She closed her eyes but her smile remained. I asked her again, "Can I ask you who I am now?"

She shook her head slowly, "Ask me later."

We lay side by side, gently touching, softly kissing. When the light vanished and the moon appeared she looked up at my window, letting the moonlight caress her hair. The stolen light of the moon shone on us and then disappeared as if on cue.

With the taste of salt still fresh on my lips and my body trembling with a delicious ache, I closed my eyes and felt her breath blow cool on my neck. When she rose off me my skin felt immediately cold and I reached out to keep her near me. She gave me a quick kiss but deftly rose despite my moan of protest.

I felt the sheet above us come away and I could only see shadows as she wrapped it about her like a cloak. She went over to the wall and found the light switch. I blinked and shielded my eyes from the sudden glare. "Hey!"

She laughed, "I don't want you to forget what I look like."

I opened my eyes and watched her as she paced the floor in front of my bed like a model walking a runaway.

"I'll never be able to forget what you look like."

Her smile broadened as her eyes went to the corner of the room where I kept some of my paintings. She went over to them quickly and knelt down. After carefully flipping the first few over she turned to me, "You're an artist?"

I shook my head, "Not really. It's only a hobby." I propped myself up on one elbow and leaned my head against my fist, "Teacher by day, tortured artist by night."

She sat down cross legged, "You don't look like a teacher."

I laughed, "It seems that I don't look like anything I am."

She smiled, "Don't be offended. You just look too young to be a teacher."

I shrugged and she asked the question that began part two. "How old are you?"

I hesitated a moment. "Twenty nine."

Her eyes opened a little wider but it only lasted a second. I could tell that it surprised her and I said, "Does that bother you?"

She wrinkled her eyebrows, "No, of course not."

I smiled, "Whew." I thought she would volunteer her age and I began to wonder if maybe she was in fact too young for me. It was at that moment that the realization hit me that I was almost thirty.

Good God. She kept smiling but said nothing. I could feel my own smile fading, "How old are you?"

She stood up and struck a pose with one hand on her hip and the other behind her head. She fluttered her eyelashes and said, "How old do you think I am?"

Twenty at the festival. Nineteen under the musky moonlight. Eighteen? I began to feel a creeping pain in my stomach. A black revelation that perhaps I really was a cradle robber. I heard my voice crack, "Nineteen?"

She beamed as if it was a compliment but her hands dropped to her side as she adjusted the sheet over her pale body. "Where do you teach?"

"Altamont. Senior Math and Biology." I said it quickly, like it didn't matter. "So, nineteen?"

She turned her back to me and went over to my CD collection, "My sister graduated from Altamont last year."

I let the question of her age simmer, "Oh? What's your sister's name?"

She picked up a CD by Iggy Pop and I cringed because it showed my age. She put it back down, "Sandra Mittendorf."

I remembered her immediately. A little heavy, sort of unkempt, but a pretty girl nonetheless. Not very popular, a great Math student, wore the same sweater every Monday. "I remember her!"

Cynthia turned and gave me a small smile.

"So, Sandra's your little sister." I said, staring a hole in the back of her head.

She straightened up gave me a challenging look. Her voice was barely a whisper, "Big sister."

I sat up, "What?"

She stuck out her chin a little and said in a clear voice, "Sandra is my older sister."

I could feel my jaw drop, "Oh my God." I covered my face with my hands and swallowed the bile that rose up my throat.

Cynthia's voice was strong and carried a touch of mocking in it, "What's wrong?"

I kept my face covered, "How old are you?"

She didn't answer and lowered my hands. I shouldn't have opened my eyes because despite the fear and revulsion, she looked beautiful. "How old are you Cynthia?"

Her blue eyes stared straight into mine, "Fifteen."

I fell back and let out a moan, "Oh my God!"

My heart raced and my arms began to shake as I covered my face again, "Oh God! I'm a pedophile!"

I felt her hands on mine, strong fingers pulling mine away. I closed my eyes tightly and her stern voice commanded me, "Open your eyes."

I did.

She kept her grip on my hands and she climbed back on top of me. I hated myself for responding to the feel of her bare thighs on mine.

"You're not a pedophile." I closed my eyes again and she almost yelled, "Look at me!"

Once again, I obeyed.

She let go of my hands and let the sheet fall off her shoulders. It fell like a rippling cascade across her shoulders. "Did you want me because I looked like a child?"

I shook my head, staring in overpowering desire mixed with self loathing.

"Did you lie to me?" Her strong voice asked.

"What do you mean?"

"When you said you loved me."

I squeezed my eyes shut and she slapped my face, "Look at me!"

My cheek burned and I saw the tears in her eyes. I didn't lie to you and I didn't lie to her either. The first of her tears landed on her breast and the second on my chest. "No, I didn't lie."

She gasped, sending more tears streaming down her cheeks, "If you loved me then, you have to love me now, because nothing has changed. I'm still me and you're still you."

I put my hand to her cheek and brushed the tears back to her neck, "Everything has changed. I made a mistake." I sucked in a breath. "I'm old enough to be your father!"

She whimpered, "And I'm old enough to be your lover."

"No," I shook my head and let go of her. "It's wrong."

She stood up suddenly and stepped off the bed. She said, "Then you're blind! And stupid! And a liar!" Each word drew blood and I wanted to take her in my arms until the world died around us.

I didn't though. Because in my mind, love like ours cannot exist. It may smolder, it may spark in a deeply hidden forge, but the flame of love can never see the light of day. It has to be quenched, if there is enough water in the world to extinguish love. It has to be yanked out, locked up and buried deep. And why? I could not answer Cynthia when she asked, nor can I answer now.

She left my room and I sucked in deep breaths of loss before I got up. I drew the sheet around me and followed her. She was already in her dress and turning the doorknob. "Cynthia..." My weak voice cried.

She turned to me and her eyes blazed, "Ask me now!"

I stood silently.

"Ask me now!"

I couldn't, because I was afraid of what she would say.

She tore open the door and left me to suffer the coldness of night. The silence bore through me and beyond the dark and the stillness, solitude dwarfed them both. Right and wrong are not mere concepts for the classroom. They gauge our every step and measure our mettle at every turn. They are immutable and carved deep into stone but they held no sway over me as my heart pounded hollow in my chest.

I went for the door, opened it, and raced down the hallway. My left hand held the sheet in place and my right clutched my breast. My bare feet tore up the thin carpet as I raced down the steps and into the dim parking lot. There, at the edge of a street light was Cynthia and when I called her name she stopped, turned and waited.

The moonlight was enough to light her form and she stood like a queen. In that moment of desperation and longing, a thought wholly alien came to me. She was Cynthia, and she was Goddess of the moon. In the stillness of the night I waited to see who I would become.

Green Sky Flood

The neighbor's kid is in my yard again. He skips over the cracks in the patio, his bare feet, wet from puddles, leave footprints that quickly vanish in the hot sun. He kneels down in the middle of the patio, in a spot that is smooth and clean and reaches into the pocket of his shorts, taking out three pieces of chalk: a yellow, a blue, a green. The he starts to make his picture.

He doesn't look up when the screen door slams behind me. I have to tip toe across the patio because it's so hot and I wonder how this kid can stand it. Every day of the summer he's out here, bare knees and elbows on the scorching concrete, oblivious to everything but the pictures he draws on my patio.

I tucked my skirt in and sat down cross legged and leaned forward, elbows on my knees, chin against my palms, watching the shapes come together in yellows, blues and greens. Willie doesn't like to talk much so I'm the first to break the silence.

"Whatcha workin' on today?"

The kid doesn't answer. He just keeps on drawing.

"Willie, what are you making?"

"A duck." He says to the ground.

"Looks good."

In about fifteen minutes the duck is clearly visible. So are the pond and the bushes and the sky. He's a pretty good artist for a 5 year old.

"Why are you making the sky green?" I stupidly ask.

"I used up the blue chalk on the pond."

"Ah."

It only takes him about ten more minutes to finish and then he sits up, cross legged like me and finally glances my way. I don't acknowledge his look because he hates that. He rests his chin on his palms, also like me, and stares down at the duck, the pond, the bushes and the sky. We sit like two sweating gargoyles for a few more minutes and then he stands up and goes to the side of the house. I turn my head and watch as he drags my watering can over, water dripping from the spout. Standing next to me with the dripping can in his hand he watches me expectantly and I say, "You can leave it. I want to look at it some more."

"You gonna wash it off after you're done?"

"Uh huh."

"OK." He sets the can down next to me and then marches off toward home, taking care not to step on the cracks.

I call after him, "See you tomorrow."

He doesn't answer. He just waves without turning around.

When I hear the gate close I turn back to the picture and watch as a caterpillar slinks along on top of the pond, toward the sky. Slowly, without any real sense of purpose, I lie down on my side to watch the caterpillar's progress. It pauses near the duck, then wanders on top of the water, circles back, then forward again. In the green sky world, the caterpillar is king. Beyond that chalky world, the grown up caterpillar on her side is too busy dreaming about being a butterfly to bother with spinning a cocoon.

When the world is empty again I stand up and take hold of the can and tip it over, washing the world away. The liquid colors melt into the pavement and I have to remember to leave a new piece of blue chalk outside. I wonder where he got the chalk that he carries in his pockets and how he is able to use them. I wonder at his wet footprints. I wonder at how he opens the gate. I'm no expert, but I thought I knew how ghosts are supposed to act.

The Extreme Middle

There is no beauty on Middleton Street. With run down tenements to the east, small retail stores on the west and nothing but garbage north and south. Wait, that's not entirely true. Sometimes, when you least expect it, a rip is made in the fabric of Middleton and a little light comes spilling in. Like the beginning of a day in August, when the sun was shining between two tenements at 5:30 in the morning.

Heading north on Middleton, just before the crest of the hill, there's an old building that used to be a youth drop in center. Before that it was a men's clothing store, and before that it was lady's shoes and a hardware store and bowler hats and petticoats and God knows what else. Tenants never stay too long on Middleton. Now the old building is an abortion clinic and that's where I work.

The building, the whole street for that matter, is deserted at the only time it looks good, and maybe that's why. Though it's a pity that no one gets to see it, except for me, because I have to be at work early. That morning I wasn't alone and beauty had two observers. A frail looking man sat on the front step smoking a cigarette and gazing into the morning sun. It was Timothy, and he was waiting for me.

He's twenty-five but doesn't look a day over eighteen. He has blonde hair, perfectly coifed and a straight toothed smile straight out of glossy pages. His clothes are wrinkled, but stylishly so, because everything about him is style. The cigarette he was holding was perfectly poised between his index and middle finger. When he raised it to his too red lips, he exhaled a stream of smoke that came out like a piece of abstract art.

He didn't look over, even when I started walking within his sight. He wanted to pose a little while longer to dazzle me with his good looks. When I reached the step I asked, "Been here long?"

He looked over at me and lifted his half-finished cigarette, now pinched between his thumb and index finger. "This long."

I nodded, but said nothing as I sat down next to him and let the sun wash over me. He didn't speak either until he flicked the cigarette toward the street. "You're early today."

"Yeah, thought I'd catch the sunrise."

"Get any sleep last night?"

I shrugged, "Maybe a couple hours."

He smiled, "That means none."

"How about you?"

He let out a delicate yawn. "I got a few hours at the motel."

"That means none."

He smiled, "Gotta make a living."

"Was it a good night?"

"Four hundred."

"Pretty good."

"Yeah, it'll go down once the kids go back to school."

I took out a cigarette of my own and lit it. "You get many students?"

"Oh yeah, except that once school starts they tend to bottle up their homosexual urges." He smiled, "Then again, maybe they just don't need me because they can hang out in locker rooms again."

"Think so?"

He took the cigarette out of my mouth and took a drag, "That's what I did."

I let my mouth curl in a way that people say makes me look cruel. "How did you manage that? You never went to school past the seventh grade."

His mouth curled into a pout, "Don't be mean." He handed the cigarette back to me, "Speaking of which, how was class last night?"

"I learned about thermodynamics."

He yawned again, "Sounds wonderful."

"You could relate to the second law."

"Oh?" He said, "What's the second law?"

"Entropy. Things moving into a state of decay."

He looked hurt, but all his looks are so practiced that it's hard to tell the real from the pretend. "Why would I like that?"

I smiled, "Because you seem to live in defiance of it. You age in reverse. I swear you look two years younger than you did last year."

He beamed. Any kind of a compliment registered glowing pleasure on his face. "That's why I make the big money sweetheart."

The sun began to creep higher in the sky and I thought about going inside to make the coffee but I didn't want to abandon Tim. We hardly saw each other anymore and it made me feel like a complete asshole whenever I brushed him off. I had nothing to say to him anymore and he never did have anything of substance to say to me. He talked about his tricks, or the shitty weather, or his tricks, or the price of cologne and clothes... or his tricks. Lately he talked about us, and I wished that he would just stick to telling me about his tricks.

"Jack, do you think my nipples are too big?"

He was fishing for a compliment and I resisted the urge to tell him that they were hideous and huge. They weren't, nothing about him was hideous. I just wanted to be mean because it seemed that I was getting good at it. I didn't say it though; not out of kindness or restraint, but because he would launch into a hurt, scorned boy tirade in his ultra feminine voice that was really starting to grate on my nerves.

"I was looking at my nipples tonight and I think they're deformed. Jack?"

I looked at the sunrise absentmindedly, "What?"

"Do you think my nipples are too big?"

"Too big?" I asked without looking at him.

"Yes, big, and flabby. I have to pinch them so they get smaller."

Without a note of conviction in my voice I said, "They're fine."

"Is that why you won't sleep with me anymore?"

I put my hand on the back of his neck and found without surprise that I dreaded the feel of his skin, "Your nipples are sublime."

He smiled thinly, accepting the praise but wanting more. "That doesn't answer my question though."

"Timmy," I always called him Timmy when I wanted to shmooze something out of him. He loved it when I called him that. "Let's not get into it this morning."

Before he could answer, a maroon Grand Marquis made its wide turn into the parking lot. We both looked over and Tim spat, "Shit, it's your mother." He leaned over, quickly kissed me on the lips and then stood up. "Call me tonight."

I gave him a wane nod, "OK."

He looked at me sternly, "Jack, I said call me tonight."

I felt my mouth begin to curl involuntarily, "I heard you. I said OK."

He gave me an impetuous sniff and then started walking north, swaying in that delicate way that made him earn 400 dollars a night.

My mother, dressed in her standard white uniform, started toward me, bending over to straighten out her nylons between steps. "Morning mom."

She motioned toward Tim with her chin, "What was he doing here?" Her voice didn't mask her scorn and it wasn't meant to. She wanted her disdain for Tim and all other homosexuals to be widely known.

"He just came by to say hello."

"Did you get tested again?"

I let out a small smile, "Yeah, last night! I got a B plus in English."

Her small eyes that I thankfully did not inherit burned fiercely, "I mean the Aids test."

I stood up with an exasperated grunt, "Yes. I tested negative for Aids but positive for leprosy."

She turned her eyes down to her purse and began fishing for her keys, "Funny boy. I'm sure we'll all be laughing ourselves sick when you show up for work with pneumonia and covered in lesions."

I took out my own keys and unlocked the front door just as she pulled her own ring of keys out. "Don't worry mom, if I wake up with lesions I'll call in sick and spare you the embarrassment."

I opened the door for her after leaning inside and flicking on the row of light switches. She strode past me, "We'll do the test right here. This week when it isn't busy."

"I was tested two months ago. Unless you can get it from a toilet seat, I'm fine."

She took off her ratty cardigan sweater and hung it up in the closet by the entrance, "If there's such a thing as an infectious toilet seat, it would belong to little Timothy."

"Did they teach you all about toilet seats and homosexuals in nursing school mom?"

It was meant to be an off hand barb, the usual substitute for normal conversation that my mother and I shared. I wasn't prepared when she suddenly whirled around to me and stuck her finger an inch away from my face. "Whatever they taught me in nursing school is moot! I haven't been a real nurse for two years! I'm a walking post hoc, pro re nata contraceptive to a city full of sluts who can't fathom the concept of a condom or God forbid, a negative reply in response to over eager sexual advances!"

I'm sure my wide eyes registered shock but my mother didn't stay to enjoy it. She turned on her heel and stormed across the white tile toward the reception desk. I quickly called out to her, "So what you're saying is I got my compassion from dad's side of the family!"

Even if that wasn't what she was saying, it had to be true. My mother was the only female misogynist on record. That's not entirely correct; classifying my mother as a hater of women would imply a specific hatred. It was my belief that mom was a misanthrope. She simply reserved a special branch of her hate for homosexuals, women who got pregnant and everyone poor.

She was smart though. Just as her lack of compassion saw fit to skip the genetic stew, her intelligence also kept clear in the makeup of her one and only fetus. I am my father's son, but that is only an assumption, as I never knew the man. He left when I was two years old and is presumably off living a life of great compassion and stupidity.

I walked slowly to the back office, letting the heels of my sneakers shuffle across the newly waxed tile. I noted a few dull spots on the floor that I had missed the night before and made a mental note to take the buffer to it after closing time.

My journey to the back of the building also revealed a burnt out florescent bulb, a wall in need of paint and a reminder to fix the gurgling sound that echoed out of the bathroom. I decided that before I set myself to any maintenance tasks I would put the coffee on and take a quick trip to the bakery three blocks over, on the more respectable Vermont Street.

I called out to the examination room that was three rooms over, "Mom! I'm going to the bakery!"

Her normally shrill voice sounded deeper, aided by the acoustics of the long hallway, "Get me a croissant!"

I yelled back that I would as I made my way to the back door and then she called out again, "Get one for Dr. Wilkes too!"

I kept walking. "He can get his own croissant! I'm not his lackey!"

"Don't be an asshole sweetie!"

Dr. Wilkes' smooth image came floating in front of me in all its handsome grandeur and a tiny thought, no bigger than a bout of insecurity, came stabbing in. I didn't want him anywhere near the bakery.

I stopped walking and called back, "OK! I'll get him one!"

I let the back door shut behind me with a metallic clang that reverberated in the thick morning air. I weaved in between the two huge dumpsters that stood like sentinels behind the clinic and then walked quickly across the back lot, past the huge wire gates that I constantly forgot to lock and into the alley, cutting through the back lots on Wilton Street. I ignored the sleeping winos and the dirty pigeons that were permanent residents of the downtown alleys.

One block further and I was in sight of Pepe's Bakery, one of my favorite places on earth. Small and made of brick, the building's large front window was always shaded by a red awning. Outside was a long box filled with flowers and an old wooden bench without a scratch or mark to mar its surface. Inside there were four small round tables with white tablecloths and a huge coffee urn set next to the glass fronted counter. More than anything else, it was the smell that made Pepe's an urban sanctuary. Fresh bread, sweet pastries, the soft, muffled aroma of flour. The heat from the ovens and the cool from a large fan bolted near the ceiling sent those smells wafting into the part of me that was still able to feel.

Pepe Jr. was the master baker, his wife Theresa was a premier pastry chef and the girl who they had practically adopted as their daughter was a child of the gods. She was twenty-one, with long black curls that would drift over her forehead. One of the most beautiful sights was those curls wiped away with the back of her flour-bleached hand.

Her name was Nell, and hearing that name spoken always made me think of an orchard in bloom or a garden full of flowers. She wore a white bakers coat and where my mother's white uniform made me think of sterility, Nell's spoke only of purity.

Brown eyes so deep that they could hold and disarm every secret in the world; it was those eyes that made my world crumble. The first time I saw her I was with Tim and he was reaching across the table to take a bite out of my cinnamon bun. I remember watching his slim fingers reach out and then I looked up and saw Nell walk in, a knapsack draped over one shoulder and a big smile for the rotund baker and his wife.

That was five months ago, when she first came to work for her Uncle Pepe and Aunt Theresa. Aside from one drunken night three years ago, she was the first woman that I had ever been attracted to. I know attraction is a broad term. We can be attracted to a house or a car just as much as to a person. What I really mean is that I fell in love with a woman after a whole life spent as a homosexual.

I didn't think it was love right away. Not with Tim's other hand on my knee. Not with a bad memory of a blonde girl from high school deeply ingrained in my psyche. Certainly not after long months of sexual insouciance. It was just a tingling at the base of my spine. It was a strange desire to hear that girl speak. To listen to her voice, her laugh, a bizarre wish to be invisible so I could watch her for days without anyone knowing. It was new and deliciously disturbing, but I wouldn't have called it love.

It was only a sexual deviation later on, when I would watch her from my table in the corner. That was the only explanation when I would study the folds of her white baker's uniform. I would sit mesmerized, watching the crease that appeared on her hip when she moved. The long, swooping lines of her back, the curve of her breasts and the milky quality of her neck were hypnotic. When her large smock slipped off her shoulder, I saw spots in the form of desire. I wanted to taste those lips and feel those curls swim beneath my fingers. I had to let my hands crawl under her clothes to get to her skin. I had to discover the secrets of her body and drink her in. Yes, it was an anomalous fling allowed to a mind that had long been under the tutelage of masculine flesh.

I mused on love, on feelings unknown, and knew that it was born when she spoke to me. When her eyes met mine in an unwavering pulse, it was love. When our casual greetings grew to long conversations over tea and bagels, it was beyond love. It was life and death and every song ever sung.

She saw me with Tim. She knew what I was and maybe it was that knowledge that made me safe to her. I was gay, and there was no threat in me. We could be friends and talk about the weather, or how our weekends were spent, or the news, or books that we had read. Even when we spoke about our families, our dreams, our pains, there was an intimate distance that I yearned to close. I loved every minute with her but I hated the safety of those talks.

I wanted to experience the danger of love. I wanted us to rush headlong into the ecstatic abyss. I wanted the delirium of romance, the rush of giggling madness, the great and mysterious dance. I coveted her, but I was not wholly selfish. I believed that my love could be made into a gift, an offering of worth. I believed that if we were together, we could both be happy.

When I opened the tinted glass door, she was there. Her smile was the greatest welcome when she saw me.

I smiled back. "Good morning!"

"Morning Jack, it looks like it's going to be a beautiful day."

Pepe came around the corner from the kitchen just at that moment. His booming voice a baritone cacophony, "Jack, your mother was here yesterday! She says I have to feed you now that you are gone from home!"

I smiled, "I've been gone from home for a year now." I patted my stomach, "I think I'm surviving quite well away from my mother's gruel."

He cocked his head, "What's gruel?"

"Bad food. She can't cook."

His voice rose again, "Don't speak bad about the mother! Never speak bad about the mother and father! That is the fifth commandment from the Lord! And even if it weren't, it is still good sense!"

My smile grew; The Lord didn't have my mother in mind when He made that rule."

He laughed, "He had all the mothers in mind!" He reached over the counter and patted my cheek with his large hand, "And He had all the rotten kids in mind too!"

Nell was giggling and the musical quality carried my eyes back to her, "How did you do on your English test?"

I looked down at the counter, brushing an imaginary crumb away, "I got a B plus."

"Holy shit! That's great!" She yelled with enthusiasm and warmth.

Theresa called from the kitchen, "Language! No bad language in here!"

Pepe grinned, "Yes, no fucking bad language here Nell."

"Pepe!" Theresa screamed.

Nell and I shared a laugh as Pepe bounced back to the kitchen to tease his wife. It was getting late and I had to be at work before the ever vigilant Dr. Wilkes arrived. He had a thing for tardiness, just like he had a thing for neatness and a thing for efficiency and a thing for everything else that was annoying to other people. I ordered three croissants and a sesame seed bun. I ordered the bun because Nell made them and as I ate I would picture her perfect little hands kneading the dough. I called my good-byes to the kitchen and then, as I always did, I took a deep breath to summon the courage necessary to profess my undying love for Nell.

"Have a great day Jack, see you at lunch."

I let the breath out in an impotent whoosh of air, "See you Nell."

The sun seemed much higher when I left the bakery and I rushed toward Middleton Street. Once there, I slowed my pace and took out the bun that Nell had made. I ate slowly, allowing my mind to spin dreams once reserved for Tim.

I walked down the very sidewalk that he walked every night. Nobody called Middleton Street by its proper name. It was Homo Hill and The Fag Strip. Young men and boys would stroll up and down, waiting for a ride. A young guy, maybe a rich older woman, maybe someone who was clean or just plain nice. Those were the hopes of the night.

I shared them once, for only one night. With images of hundred dollar bills and fed with funny, severely edited stories by Tim, I was hopeful and eager my first night on Middleton. I had to be, because I was there for my son.

Three years ago at a drunken party, I had one too many swigs from the communal bottle of Jim Bean and took a liking to a girl with cute blonde locks and a tiny smile. Her name was Helen and she slurred that I was beautiful. One night, one entanglement, one baby born prematurely eight months later. Adam, the first-born. It was because of my son that I stood on the dark street and dreamed of making enough money to take him away with me.

It was a noble cause, banishing all fear. I thought that I could do whatever the customer wanted with closed eyes and a mind far away. When the blue station wagon pulled up beside me I only saw lucre. Hopes and dreams and tailor made seams on the fabric of my visions. The fat man in the station wagon was going to help me.

He leaned over and opened the door for me, giving me a big smile and displaying the black gums that come from chewing tobacco. His index finger was like a sausage, bending in a come hither gesture meant to be seductive. If there's money involved, there's no need for seduction, but even fat guys with bad gums need a victory. They need to feel that I'm coming along for them and not just the money so I smiled sweetly before I got in the car.

He had two twenties sitting on top of the dashboard. "Can I get head for that?" His smile faltering as he asked.

"A blow job is fifty." I said, trying to sound halfway tough like I've been on the streets for yonks.

"All's I got is forty." He said as he put the car in drive.

I kept the door open. "It's fifty."

He pressed his foot down hard on the brake and dug his fat hand into his jean pocket. "Alright, I got another ten in here."

I took the money from his hand and along with the two twenties off the dashboard, I put it into my pocket. I smiled, "Where do you want to do this?"

He took his foot off the brake and I closed the door. We drove a few blocks south on Middleton and then he took a right, heading for the Ninth Street overpass that led to an industrial area. It was a favorite spot for nocturnal adventures as all the empty warehouses and dark side streets provided a modicum of privacy.

We didn't speak until he pulled behind a storage lot. He put the car in park and smiled, reaching out his ham hock of a hand to my face. His hand was greasy and moist and I pushed my mind into a safe place. Watching a movie with Tim, laughing over the plot and characters. The sunset over Westglen Park. A pizza from Delbaggios...

He had his hand around my head and he was squeezing, moving my head around as his hips rose to meet me. I pulled back and tried to be coy, "You don't have to grab my ears, I know what I'm doing."

Just as I was about to go back down his hand slapped me, "I'll touch you any way I want, you goddamn fairy!"

I was shocked and didn't react until he slapped me again. Then I put a stereotype to bed. I leaned back out of his reach and then shot out my right fist, connecting with the soft flab of his cheek. His head snapped back and before he could move I hit him two more times, drawing blood from his nose and lip.

He was dazed as I leaned over and opened up the driver's door, kicking him out onto the asphalt. He was struggling to get his pants pulled up but I was out his door and over him in a second. I kicked him repeatedly in the back and neck. "Did you think I was your little girl you fat piece of shit?"

I kicked him in the back of the head and his forehead smacked the pavement.

He lay still, moaning softly, and I reached into his pants and took out his wallet. There was no money inside, no credit cards and no pictures of a wife and kids. I flipped through it and came up with a laminated birth certificate, his driver's license and a gift certificate for a free egg Mcmuffin. "You're just poor white trash aren't you fat boy?"

He began to shake a little, making the rolls of fat around his exposed waist shake. He began to sniff and snort, his body displaying the embarrassment and humiliation. I turned away, grabbed the keys out of the ignition and threw them over the chain link fence about twenty feet away.

"A nice walk will do you some good. Vent out some of that anger you have."

I threw his wallet down on top of him and started the long quiet walk back to Middleton.

I never walked the street again. I was furious with Tim. He warned me, but he didn't warn me well enough because if he had, I would have never set foot on the sidewalk. I took the money out of my pocket and threw that to the wind as well. I would have to see my dreams come true the hard way and little Adam would have to wait.

My experience was tame compared to the stories that I've heard. Tim himself had told me of at least a half dozen near rapes and assaults to keep me awake at night. I knew guys, mere boys of fourteen and fifteen, tell me in their war hardened voices about being tied up for days at a time or being stabbed with Exacto knifes and cut open with shards of glass.

It was sickening and saddening, but I was powerless to change it. It wasn't fair, but where is justice given to the so-called ruck of humanity? I couldn't even stop Tim from going out night after night. He loved the rush, the thrill and of course, the money. Back when I cared, I would lay awake at night and look at the scars on his little body and wondered at what price those thrills had come.

He wasn't like the drug addicts, who had to do it or suffer inconceivable withdrawal pain. He wasn't a kid, with nowhere to go. He was a full-grown man in a kid's body, but that was only the outside. Inside he was a sweet and caring person. He could be tough, and chances are he would get tougher as the years passed. Inside he was weak, though he could brag about a hundred escapes from certain death. Inside he was lonely, though hundreds desired him. Inside was the opposite of outside, but I knew that soon they would meet in a dirty equilibrium.

     I finished my bun and looked down at the crumbs on my shirt ruefully. The street that I had walked on drove away my dreams of Nell. It was too late to get them back as I saw that all cars were present in the clinic's staff parking lot.

     I went in through the back door and brought my mother her croissant. Dr. Wilkes came around a corner a second later, "Jack, that toilet sounds like it's about to give birth."

I smiled. "We're having a pool for sex and weight. Do you want in?"

The pedantic doctor looked at me blankly, "Why do I keep you around here?"

I handed him the paper bag I was holding, "To get you croissants."

He took the bag and peeked inside, "Croissants? Is that what you people..."

He stopped short and I lifted an eyebrow in preparation.

He cleared his throat, "Alright, you're forgiven. But please get that toilet fixed this morning."

"Will do, doc." I gave him a crisp salute and then walked past him to the supply closet.

     I spent the morning fixing the toilet and sitting outside smoking with Gelda and Marie, the women who cleaned the place. They were the only two people there that Dr. Wilkes didn't complain about. With good reason too, as I had been working there for over a year and had never once seen a drop of blood.

"Nurse Claire, she's a crazy." Gelda said at our ten o'clock smoke break.

"She's nice. Why do you say she's crazy?" I asked.

Gelda made a face indicating extreme impatience for my ignorance. "You know why she work here?"

"Because she's a nurse?"

"No, you stupid. She work here to pray for the babies!"

"What?"

She leaned closer to me, allowing me a good whiff of her salami and dill pickle on rye that she had just finished, "She told me she work here to pray for the babies. She say, 'who else gonna pray for these babies?' She a crazy."

Marie nodded, but remained silent.

I shrugged, "That doesn't mean she's crazy."

Gelda let out a snort, "You tell me a woman who work at an abortion clinic should be praying for the babies? Dr. Wilkes say they no even babies. I say yes, they babies, but OK, that's for the momma to decide whether she keep or not."

Marie nodded.

Gelda gave me a stiff poke in the arm, "What you think? They babies or no?"

I never got into those kinds of discussions so I said, "Whatever I think has nothing to do with Nurse Claire praying. I think it's kinda nice."

"Ach, nice! It's crazy! She want to pray for the babies she should get a picket sign like the others and march up and down the street."

Marie nodded; throwing her cigarette out into the gravel that covered our back lot.

The door opened behind us and my mother came out, "Jacksie, give your momma a cigarette. I need some relief."

I gave her one and Gelda said, "Liza, what you think about Nurse Claire?"

My mother threw her head back as she inhaled. A forty-year-old Marlene Deitrich, that was my mom. "Claire is a good nurse."

"Ya, but she a crazy right?"

My mother looked at Gelda as she was looking at a turd, "You spend your life cleaning toilets. What right do you have criticizing a professional?"

Gelda dropped her head and looked at her hands.

She had upset me with her thoughts on Nurse Claire, who was the closest thing to an angel that Middleton Street had ever seen. Of course, seeing Gelda berated and insulted by the queen of all bitches was another story altogether. Sometimes it's hard to feel pity for people that you disdain, but watch them after ten seconds with my mother and you'll discover reams of unused compassion.

Marie stood up and went inside without speaking and Gelda followed.

I turned to my mother, "That was cruel."

She kept her eyes on the street. "I was merely sticking up for Claire."

"No you weren't. Gelda called Claire a nut and then you called Gelda an ignorant washwoman. That's straight out of the schoolyard. I thought you were more mature than that."

She flicked her cigarette away the same way Tim did, with a quick, fluid motion. "Sonny, once you've seen as much as me then you can do some lecturing. Until that time, study hard at school so you don't have to fix toilets for the rest of your life."

She went inside without another word or glance toward me. I waited a few seconds and then went inside so I could change the light ballast before I went back to Pepe's for my lunch date.

Dr. Wilkes was just coming out of the operating room and without even looking at me said, "Jack, that light needs changing."

Before I could answer he went into his office, where an attractive young woman was sitting in front of his desk.

I got the ladder and the replacement ballast and set everything up right by the reception desk, where Clara Jones spent forty hours a week. She smiled when I started climbing the ladder, "Thank God, that humming was about to drive me insane."

In the waiting room were three women. Two of them were in their late teens and the other was an older, dignified woman reading Cosmopolitan. The two girls looked scared out of their minds and every time they looked up Clara gave them a warm smile.

Clara has the best smile on record. She's about sixty years old and she always wears a smilie face button. Her dentures, when exposed by her beaming smile, show that a few of them are a little crooked and stained. Still, nobody wants to see a row of perfect teeth in a smile, it's just too intimidating. Clara's smile makes you want to smile right back. It brightens up a room and invites everyone in. She's a great old bird.

She picked up the beeping phone and listened for a moment. "Jack, it's Helen."

I had a mess of wires around my head like an electric wig so I spoke into the dust of the acoustic ceiling. "Can you take a message please? I don't want to electrocute myself up here."

I heard her tell the mother of my son that I was busy and then she listened for a few seconds before hanging up. "She says she'll be dropping by in an hour."

"Shit! That's right on my lunch break!"

I could hear Clara smile, "Well, that's why she's coming then. She doesn't want to bother you in the middle of work."

I screwed the new ballast in place, "Aw, who gives a shit about work? I don't want to miss my lunch break."

Just then I heard Dr. Wilkes underneath me, "That's a fine attitude you've got there Jack. Ever think of becoming a motivational speaker?

I pushed the wires off my head and looked down at my boss, "Doc, that's almost funny. There's hope for you yet."

He ignored me as he guided the young lady that was in his office out the door. I watched him smile at the two teenagers as he strode by. Both of the girls watched as his white coat fluttered at the tails as his long strides carried him to the door.

By the time I was done rewiring and putting all my tools away, it was a few minutes before twelve. I decided to wait for Helen on the front step as the sight of her sent my mother into hysterics. You would think that seeing a person who had led me astray on the sexual orientation path would be the delight of her eyes but Helen seemed to typify everything that my mother hated: young, poor and a single mother. My mom hated women like Helen more than those who chose to terminate their pregnancies. "Just another poor brat added to the list. How can any decent person bring a child into this world?"

My mother is an absolute when it comes to hate but she's a walking contradiction when it comes to why she hates.

I sat on the step and alternated looking from my watch to the street, anxious to get the time spent with Helen out of the way so I could go see Nell. I didn't despise Helen. She was, after all, the one who gave life to my son. My dislike comes from knowing that because of her coquettish smile I ended up a father. I'm also a walking contradiction thanks to my mother's side of the family.

I wasn't sitting long before the front door opened and Nurse Claire Swathers came out. She tucked her skirt underneath her as she sat down, "Mind if I share the view with you?"

"Sure Claire, out for some degenerate sight seeing?"

She sucked on her lip in a gesture of disapproval and then said, "You don't look too well Jack. Are you still having trouble sleeping?"

I nodded, "I just don't want to miss any of those great infomercials."

She laughed, "Just tape them so you can get some sleep."

I watched her as she laughed, and it was only at those times that she became moderately attractive. Claire Swathers was a terrific human being, but all things being equal, she really got short changed in the looks department. She had sallow skin, bad teeth and a twisted nose. I thought it was by divine grace that her husband could have been a model. He was a handsome man who must have fallen in love with Claire's soul because as far as my penetrating eye could see, her heart was all she had.

"Claire, can I ask you something?"

"Shoot."

"Why do you work here?"

She gave me a confused look, "Because I'm a nurse."

"Yeah," I said, "But you don't approve of what goes on here. You're not pro-choice."

She pursed her lips and looked up for a moment as if gathering her thoughts. "I don't really care about being pro-choice or pro-life. I work here because I think someone should care about the babies. They deserve a prayer at least once in their lives. I also work here because I care about the women. They're not doing something easy. They've made a hard choice and need reassurance and caring. They deserve a prayer too."

"What about the two timers and the three timers who act like they don't give a shit?"

Claire looked at me solemnly, "They do give a... a care. They hide it and try to act strong and cold but you can see, when they're on the table and they close their eyes to hide their pain." She took a deep breath, "Their souls are crying and they need to be loved, because whether they made a mistake or not, they deserve love and forgiveness. I work here for them, because it doesn't matter what I believe or what choices I've made, it could be me in their shoes." I looked at her but she was staring straight ahead and her hands were fists. "We have the freedom to chose, but freedom can be the heaviest burden any of us have to carry."

I looked down at the step. "My mother works here because she can't get a job at a hospital. You should pray for her too Claire."

"I do Jack. Your mom has a lot of pain inside." She smiled, "It's not easy being a bitch all the time."

We laughed and then I gave her a kiss on the cheek. She immediately blushed and straightened out her skirt with a furrowed brow.

"You really are a good person, Claire."

She looked up, "So are you Jack." She stared at my face for a second or two and then asked, "You believe that, don't you?"

I felt myself blush and I turned away.

We sat silently until Helen and her fiancé drove up. The black Saab was newly washed and waxed and I could say the same thing about her fiancé's hair. He was a lawyer with a large firm downtown and despite his pretentious bearing; I knew that he would be good for Helen. She looked freshly made up too, presumably because the courtship was still on and she was waiting until the gold band was on her finger before she went out shopping in her bath robe and curlers.

They parked at the farthest end of the parking lot and Helen walked over to me alone. As I left Claire on the step I noticed immediately that Adam wasn't with Helen. I asked her where he was before I even said hello.

"He's at day care."

"How's the asthma?"

"Persistent, but manageable."

I nodded, and looked around absentmindedly until she decided to tell me why she was there.

"Tony got a job in Boston."

I nodded, waiting for the punch line.

"So obviously Adam and I are going too."

I gave an incredulous smile, "Uh Helen, we have to talk about that. I mean, I'm Adam's father. I should have a say in this."

She shook her head. "There's nothing to talk about. We're leaving next month and that's it."

I could feel my face flush, "Helen, don't make me go ballistic here. We're talking about my son!"

Her eyes bore into me, "I know we're talking about Adam. What would you have me do? Break off the best chance that your son will ever have?"

"Don't you mean the best chance you'll ever have?"

Her voice cracked as it rose, "Yes dammit, I mean that too! And there's no way I'm giving this up. I love Tony, Tony loves me and Tony loves Adam too."

I let out a guffaw. "Tony loves Adam so he can get in your pants."

Her eyes were blazing, "We are not discussing that!"

I sighed and turned away, walking a few steps before turning back. I held out my hands, "Helen, you're talking about taking my son away from me. I can't afford to move to Boston. I'm in school now and... shit! Think how that makes me feel."

"If you love Adam, you'll let us go with your blessing. Tony is going to buy us a house in the suburbs, away from the smog and the smell and the shit. You know that this is the best for Adam."

"I do love him, that's why I can't let you do this!"

She stepped closer to me and her voice sank to a hiss, "Don't you talk about love for Adam! You're the one that wanted me to get an abortion! You're the one that didn't even want him born!"

I yelled, "Well I want him now! If you want to go off to Boston with that asshole, then that's fine. Just leave Adam with me."

She laughed hoarsely, "Oh yeah, that would work. So you and your little fag friend can raise my son? I'd sooner have aborted him than have him grow up to be one of you people!"

I could feel my jaw drop. Helen had expressed shock over who I was initially, but she had never voiced that kind of opinion before. I was completely incredulous and couldn't speak.

Her voice softened, "Jack, I'm sorry. But you have to realize that you taking care of him on your own isn't even an option."

I couldn't even raise my eyes from her knees. I had never felt so utterly powerless, so completely impotent in all my life. I knew there was no way I could fight it. I loved Adam but he was leaving, along with the only dream that I had ever had. I would have built a house for him and me in the country. I would have saved every penny and taken him away with me. I saw the little house and the trees and Adam playing in the yard but that image blew softly away when Helen spoke.

"Jack, look at me." She sighed when I did look at her. "I know you love Adam. Can you ever doubt that I don't?"

"No, of course not but..."

"I love him more than my own life. I want what's best for him. I know you do too. You'll see him, you'll visit or we'll visit. I'm not taking him away from you. I'm trying to give him a better life."

She cupped my chin and kissed my forehead, "We leave in two weeks. I hope you can understand."

I nodded, feeling a tiny bit comforted that I could see her love for our son.

She stepped away and went back to the idling car, "I'll bring Adam by on the weekend."

I nodded again and waved, feeling like a widow watching the ships sail.

Claire had remained on the steps and it was obvious that she had heard it all. She stood up when I approached and put her arms around me. I couldn't hug back because I wasn't ready to let go. I needed that pain, because it made me real. I was less than half a father to Adam. I saw him on the odd weekends and changed his diapers and kissed his tummy to make him giggle. I sat cross-legged on the carpet with him and made noises with stuffed animals. I fretted and worried when he had an asthma attack but I wasn't a father.

I was twenty-one years old and taking English and science courses at night without ever really knowing why. I had no career, no plans beyond the pipe dream of a home away from the smog and the street and all the people who chose sides and played on teams in a game that I cared nothing for. I was barely a man, much less a father.

Claire held me tighter but I just stood there, my arms hanging limp and wishing that I could cry. I wish I could do something, something, something, anything. The door opened in front of me and it was my mother, standing there with one hand on the door handle and the other on her hip, "Sorry to break up the twelve step program, but there's a toilet barfing water all over the place."

Claire finally released me and turned to the doorway, "Liza, Jack just found out that Helen and Adam are moving to Boston."

My mother did her best at showing sympathy and that was by giving a low whistle and then saying, "Well Jack, you know that you and Timothy weren't a good influence anyway. It's for the best."

I wanted to scream but I kept my voice low, "You don't really give a shit. You never wanted to see your own grandchild. You never held him, not once."

Her eyes seemed to burn. "I want no part of your mistakes. I don't need to cuddle a reminder of your failures."

"Mom." I said weakly.

Her chin raised, "Yes Jack?"

I moved past her. "Fuck you."

I went to the supply closet to get a plunger and I managed to unplug the toilet without thinking about anything except not getting my feet wet. I mopped up the water and brought the plunger back to the tiny room. It was there, with the heat and closeness of the room that I broke down. I kicked the door shut behind me and sat down on the floor with my head in my hands. I cursed and I cried. I could feel my body shake with each sob but it was a distant, alienating feeling. I was above myself, floating at the ceiling and watching my pathetic shell crying and muttering.

Chained to a wandering breeze, I felt that I never knew who or what I was. I didn't know what to believe or even what to opine. I didn't know which category I fit in, which group I should side with or whether I could be left or right. I was stuck in the middle, straddling a fence with eyes roaming back and forth. Love and hate, black and white and all other solid, real things were beyond me.

It was years melted into minutes by the time I stood up. I wiped my eyes on the sleeve of my work shirt and took five deep breaths. Five seconds in, hold for five more, five seconds out. Magic five, a magical time.

I walked out of the closet and my mom and Claire were nowhere in sight. The face that greeted me was that of Dr. Wilkes. "Your little episode over now?"

I stared at him blankly before I gave a slow nod.

"A girl was here to see you but we didn't want to interrupt your quality time."

"Who? Who was here?"

"Pretty girl, from the bakery. What's her name, Nell?"

A part of me was thankful that she hadn't seen me in my state but another, more powerful part felt a stab of regret.

"She a friend of yours?"

I nodded again.

He was smiling lewdly, "Very pretty girl."

I felt my eyes narrow.

"I'll have to take a trip down to that bakery."

My voice quavered, "She's not your type Wilkes."

He laughed, "Well, she's certainly not your type."

I took a quick look around to see if there were any patients nearby. The coast was clear so I smiled, "Wilkes, why don't you stick to banging your patients. Stay away from the bakery."

His face contorted into pure wrath. His words came out slowly, "What did you just say to me?"

I leaned closer to him, "I said, you better fire me now before I spread the word around the waiting room about how you're a philandering, quasi pedophile."

He sputtered but I spoke again, "Maybe you should just go to the single bars instead of doing trial runs in the O.R. But then again, you don't get a sneak peek at the goods in the bars do you doctor?"

His fist reared back and I put my face even closer, "Please do it doc, please."

He lowered his fist and took a small step back.

"I'll come back to get my tools."

I walked to Westglen Park and sat on a bench, watching a squirrel for the better part of two hours. At seven o'clock the bakery would close and I would be there, to see Nell. I would tell her the truth. I would tell her all truths.

The squirrel that I had been watching leapt down from a tree and tore across the grass. In its absence came Tim, with a change of clothes and a small smile. I let out a sigh at he approached and I thought back to when seeing him would always bring a smile to my face. Protected and protector, I used to find all in him. Something fell away in that time and as I sat on the bench, I only felt wanted. I no longer felt loved.

His smile remained in place when he sat down. It was a sympathetic smile, a pity smile, a lean on me and I'll see you through smile. "I heard about Adam."

"Who told you?"

"The ugly nurse at the clinic."

"Claire?"

"Yeah, the one with the fucked up nose."

"She's not ugly."

He turned away, his smile disappearing and his self-serving battle plan crumbling. "Anyway, I'm sorry about Adam. We could have raised him right, you and me."

I let out a half laugh, half guffaw.

He looked back to me. "What was that supposed to mean?"

I smiled, trying to soften the blow, "Tim, you always took off when Adam was around. You have no parental instincts whatsoever. You're still a child yourself."

"Oh, and you're not?"

I shook my head. "I am too. I was too young to be a father and when I became one, I wasn't very good at it. Chances are I wouldn't have got much better."

He put his hand on the back of my head. "Don't say that Jack. You love Adam. That's all that's expected of a father."

I said, "Well, I wouldn't know."

His fingers began to twirl a lock of my hair, "Me neither. That's why you and I have to learn all these things from each other. Just like we always have."

His hand went to the back of my neck and he kissed me softly under my ear. "We'll teach each other." He whispered as his other hand rode up my leg.

"Tim, stop."

"No." He whispered, flicking his tongue along my neck as he leaned closer to me. "You and I are like twins. We're both afraid of the dark."

I thought about my long nights. Sitting in a chair with all the lights on, afraid to let the dark creep over me.

"I don't want to be afraid anymore." I said softly.

His hand was near my crotch and he began to grind against me, "We don't have to be afraid as long as we have each other."

"Stop it Tim."

He kept on. "I love you Jack." Then his hand began to undo my zipper.

I stood up. "Tim, I said stop."

He looked up at me with a look of frustration before he leaned back, both arms draped over the back of the bench, "What's wrong Jack? Is it me? Do I disgust you?"

The answer was yes but I shook my head, "No Timmy, I just..."

He quickly leaned forward, "Is it someone else?"

My silence said that it was.

"You fucker. You son of a bitch!"

"Timmy, please..."

"Don't...call me that. Just don't. We always said that we'd be open with each other. We always swore to communicate." He stood up, facing me. "If you had just talked to me! Maybe we could have worked this out. Maybe you wouldn't have had to two-time me! Maybe I could have stopped you from being a whore like everyone else."

I rolled my eyes, "Spare me the hysterics Tim. Hypocrisy doesn't suit you very well. You're out on the street every night giving blowjobs to a hundred different guys. Don't talk to me about fidelity."

He narrowed his eyes. "As soon as I stop charging you can call me a hypocrite. I only loved you, you asshole. I never even fell asleep with another man. There's no way you can compare what I do to those men to what you and I have."

I sighed, "I'm sorry. I was out of line."

He sat back down and lowered his head, "Oh fuck."

We remained silent for a few seconds before his head shot up again, "Is it Andy? That pizza boy slut from Delbaggio's? Oh please tell me it isn't him!"

I shook my head. "It isn't Andy."

"Who then? Alex? I see how he looks at you. He's filthy! He's a complete moron!"

I let out a breath, "It isn't Alex, it isn't Andy. It's Nell."

He squinted at me, "Who's Neil?"

"Not Neil. Nell. From the bakery. I'm in love with Nell."

He looked at me blankly for second or two and then he started to laugh.

I kept staring at him until he stopped. Even then he didn't seem believe me. "Nell's a girl."

I said dryly, "How very observant."

He returned the smile, "I've got a news flash for you Jackie. You're gay."

"Am I?" I looked at him with pleading, "I don't want to be defined by who I sleep with and I can't be defined by who I love. Why can't we just fall in love with anyone? Like when you and I loved each other."

I saw his eyes begin to mist, "I still love you Jack. Don't talk about my feelings for you in the past tense." He stood up again, taking both of my hands in his. "I still love you and I think that deep down you love me too. You're just confused..."

I let go of his hands. "Of course I'm confused!"

I sat down on the ground with my legs folded underneath. "I love her Timmy. I love her and I don't know what to do."

He sat down next to me but wisely did not touch me. "You always were a strange one Jack. You and I have a fight and then you have a fling with Helen, changing your life forever. Then me again. Now this Nell girl. You don't know what you want. You just don't know who you are."

I looked at him sadly, "I never meant to hurt you Timmy. I really do love you. We'll always be friends."

He laughed, "Oh, the 'we'll always be friends' line. I hate that shit Jack. No one can be content with friendship if once they were lovers."

"I'm sorry. I wish you could know how sorry I am."

He smiled, running his hand down my cheek. "I hope you can get straightened out."

I laughed, "Good choice of words."

He kept smiling and then he took my face in both hands and kissed me on the lips, "When you find out who you are, call me."

He stood up and quickly walked away the same way that he had come. I stayed on the grass for a while longer. I felt empty, but it was a good kind of emptiness. I wasn't bereft of blessings, I was simply waiting to be filled with them. I had my supper at a hot dog stand and my dessert at Baskin Robbins. When the warm breeze from the south cooled, I knew it was time to see Nell.

I arrived at the bakery just when she was walking out. She looked startled when she saw me and before anything was spoken she hugged me. Her hair was soft against my cheek and it smelled sweet. I was aware of every part of her that touched me. Her breasts against my chest, her legs touching mine, and her arms around me. I thought that it had to be fate, because she knew that I loved her. I pulled her closer to me, feeling the soft firmness of her lower back.

She let go. "I'm so sorry to hear about Adam."

It was like a weight being put back on my chest. She hadn't come to me out of love. It was pity.

I nodded, "Thanks. But, I know it's for the best and I'll get to see him on holidays and maybe I needed this time to grow. I don't know." I smiled, "All the positive things and that other rot."

She smiled, "Things will work out for the best."

We stood two feet apart, her face starting to look a little uncomfortable. "So, have you told Tim yet?"

I nodded, "He knows. Um, Nell. I came here..."

She smiled, inviting me in.

"I came here to tell you that I love you."

Her smile faltered, "I... well, that's very sweet of you." She added quickly, "I love you too."

I took a step toward her, "I mean I love you. Flowers and candy and Romeo under the balcony kind of love." I took her hands. "I'm IN love with you."

She didn't speak but it looked like she was going to say about ten different things but stopped each time. She let out a small, nervous laugh. "I don't know what to say."

"You don't have to say anything. I just wanted you to know." I turned my face away. "I wanted you to know how I feel about you."

"Jack," she said with a look of complete piety, "I love you as a friend. I never thought of you in any other way because... well, because."

"Because you thought I was gay."

She smiled, "You're not gay?"

"No. I'm nothing. I'm a man. I love you. That's all I understand."

Her smile remained as she blew out a little gust of air, "Well, that changes things. I mean, I like you and all. Maybe someday..."

"Maybe someday..." I nodded to myself.

She spoke quickly, "Yes, maybe someday. Maybe, but right now, let's be friends. Let's be good friends and see what happens."

A car pulled up and inside was a handsome young man. The passenger window glided down at the flick of a button, "Sorry I'm late."

She turned to me with lips held tight together before she spoke. "That's my ride."

I could feel hope slipping away yet again. Indeed, Nell and I would be friends because that's all we could be. I waved to the handsome reason sitting in the car. The guy looked at me suspiciously before giving me a brief wave.

"I should go." Nell said.

I smiled as best I could, "Yeah, see you around."

She touched my cheek. "I'll see you tomorrow. Uncle Pepe's letting me make the croissants. I'll make one just for you."

I nodded, "I'll be here."

She kissed me on the cheek quickly and then got in the car. My skin was still tingling by the time they disappeared around the corner.

I let out a sigh and then I heard Pepe's voice behind me. "Jack. You sit with me?"

I turned around and saw that he was already lowering himself onto the bench.

He began to fill his pipe and as I sat down next to him he said, "I heard about Adam. Nell told Theresa and me. You feel bad?"

I smiled, looking out at the quiet street. "I feel bad for a million different reasons."

"Nah, don't feel bad. Adam has trouble with breathing, yes?"

I nodded, "Asthma."

"Yeah, and maybe he go to a nice place so he no breathe bad anymore."

"Maybe."

"Yeah, this city no good. Bad air. Cars, factories, old men with the pipes."

I smiled and he continued, "So it's good he get better maybe."

"Yeah, that's the good part."

He blew out a thin stream of smoke, "That's love. You give up a little bit for the love."

"It's giving up a lot."

"Sometimes," He said, "The more you love, the more you have to give up."

I didn't reply and he smoked silently for a few minutes before he said, "You love Nell."

I was surprised that he knew and I nodded slowly, "Yes."

He nodded back as if agreeing with himself, "I see that. Theresa, she see right away. She got good eyes."

"I wish Nell could see it."

"Oh, she see. She love you too. She care a lot about you."

"Yeah, as a friend."

He spoke forcefully, "Yeah, as a friend! That's love too!"

"It's not the kind I want. I want her to love me the way I love her. I want to make her happy."

He pointed down the street with his pipe. "What if that boy in the car make her happy?"

"Then I'm fucked."

"Yeah, then you fucked. But you know what else it mean?" He didn't wait for my answer, "It mean that you no love her at all! You love somebody then you want them happy."

"I know." I said softly.

"You know? Do you?"

I stood up, "Ah shit Pepe, I don't know anything! I don't even know who I am!"

He smiled, "I know you. You Jack, now sit down so I don't hurt my neck looking up at you."

I sat back down and he said, "Yeah, nobody know who they are. Maybe you go on that Oprah show and she tell you who you are, eh?"

"Maybe."

"Ach, everybody want to be something. Look at that place you work. What do you call them people with the signs? What do you call them?"

"The protestors? They're Pro life."

"Yeah yeah, pro life. And the others? The ones that argue with them?"

"Pro choice."

"Yeah, and now what you call that Timothy?"

"Tim? What do you mean?"

"What is he?"

"Uh, a homosexual?"

"Yeah, a homosexual. Now what you say that Obama is?"

"The president?"

"No, no, a democrat. The other guys are republicans. Yes?"

"Yeah."

"Now, the postman. What he?"

"Well, he's black."

"Yes, yes, he's black. And Mr. Chu, he is a Vietnamese." He closed his eyes halfway and spoke softly, as if to himself. "What else is different with people? Clara, the woman at work, she is a widow. Mr. Heinz, the cop, he is in that church, the one about no church on Sunday. And Mr. Ahmed, he go to the mosque. And Maria, she is from Puerto Rico. You can look at the skin, or the church they go to, or what they do… you don't have to look hard to find what make them different from you." He turned his eyes on me, "Now what you?"

"I'm white. A Caucasian."

"Ach! No, you dummy! What you?"

"Uh, I don't know what you mean."

"Listen to me now you dummy. Take the pro life and the pro choice and the homosexuals and the blacks and the yellows and the old and the young and the tall and the short and take the dummies like you and stick them all in a room." He peered out into the street for effect, "Then you look at them all and ask, who are they? You tell me, who are they?"

"Uh, people?"

"Yes! People! That's it! You don't got to go farther than that! The beaver is the beaver and he eats wood. The cow is the cow and he makes milk and the bear is the bear and he shits in the woods." He laughed, "Only the people, they forget they people! They think all the time, 'who am I? What do I think about? What do I believe? What make me different? Who am I? Who am I?' Ach, they people! Who gives a fuck?" He looked at me solemnly, "Jack, you just be Jack. Who gives a shit what you believe? Who cares what side of the street you live on? Just be Jack and be happy with being Jack. That's all you gonna be anyway, just Jack. Like me, I'm Pepe, always, all the time, forever."

He thumped his chest, "Pepe." Then he hit me in the chest with the flat of his hand. "Jack." He leaned back and sucked a mouthful of smoke and then let it out as he spoke, "That's it."

I nodded like I understood and then I sighed.

"You still feel bad eh? About that guy in the car with Nell."

I nodded slowly and sighed, breathing in the aromatic smoke from his pipe.

He smiled as if he were the only one in on a joke. Then he tapped my arm, "Hey dummy, you know what else you don't know?"

"What's that?"

"That guy in the car, who come get Nell." I waited, watching his smile grow. "That's her brother!" Then he started laughing so hard that he gave himself a coughing fit. Once he regained his breath he patted my leg, "Now, let's you and me enjoy this sunset. You know, a sunset is only a sunrise saying, 'I'll see you later.'"

He told me about sunsets, and about pigeons and winos and why Detroit wasn't making good cars anymore. He lectured and opined. He made jokes that made himself laugh. I laughed along, and watched as the smoke from his pipe drifted into the evening.

Pictures worth a Thousand Words

EXT: Los Angeles, Outside a Motel Room

Cut to:

An attractive woman in her mid thirties. She is smiling, but looks tense. Behind her stands a younger, also attractive woman, in her twenties. They are looking at me, an older gentleman in his late forties.

Helen: Aren't you going to invite us in?

Me: I wasn't planning on it.

INT: A Dirty Motel Room

The two women step inside and the younger of the two closes the door. Helen casts a deprecating eye around the filthy hotel room as she takes off her coat and hands it to her assistant.

Cut to:

The assistant as she looks around for a closet or a coat hook and after a moment folds the coat over her arm. Helen knocks some empty fast food containers off a table and puts her purse down. Her disgusted expression remains as she looks back to me, wearing only a yellow terry cloth robe and white socks.

Helen: You look dashing as always.

I walk past her to the writing table that is set up near the window. I take out a cigarette from a crumpled pack of Marlboro's and light it.

Me: (Exhaling smoke) If I'd known you were coming I'd have worn some underwear.

Helen: If you'd answer the phone once in a while you would've known I was coming over.

Me: (Looking away absentmindedly) I've been busy.

Helen: So the script is done?

Me: Not exactly.

I squint at the assistant.

Me: Who are you?

Helen: Jenny, my assistant.   You've only met her twenty times before.

Me (to Jenny): Nice to meet you.

Helen goes over to the writing table and looks down at the typewriter that has sat dormant for the last week.   Next to the typewriter sits the unedited script.

Helen: How much do you have left to do?

Helen stands close enough that I can smell her perfume.   It smells nice, but I'm nto on speaking terms with nice things so I walk over to the bed and sit down.   Jenny remains standing near the door with Helen's overcoat still folded over her arm.

Me: Oh, just a few pages to go.

Helen: What do you call a few?

Me: I dunno, about a hundred.

Helen: (With an expression rapidly turning from disgust to anger) Charlie, don't fuck around!

I reach over to the night table in an attempt to flick the ashes from my cigarette into the ashtray and end up missing.

Cut to:

The ashes falling on the floor.

Me: (Smiling) I'm not fucking around. I have about a hundred pages to go.

Helen: (Anger fully evident) It was supposed to be on Dennison's desk on Monday!

Me: And I was supposed to be a Nobel Prize winner. 'Supposed to" is an impotent statement. It means absolutely nothing.

Helen: Does the Pulitzer mean nothing?

Me: Fuck the Pulitzer. And don't give me a pep talk. I'm beyond needing pep.

Helen: Don't pull this shit on me now Charlie! I need that script! My ass is on the line here!

Me: I'm sure your ass will find its way off the line without much trouble,

Helen: (Anger again) I need that fucking script!

Me: Helen, get a hold of yourself. It's not the end of the world. It's a movie for God's sake. (Standing) Let me fix you a drink. (To Jenny) Want a drink?

Jenny shakes her head quickly.

Me: Helen?

Helen: I don't want a drink! (Pause) Are you drunk?

I go over to the bureau and take the half empty bottle of Jim Bean in my hand.

Me: A little. Just a little mind you.

Helen: It's ten thirty in the morning! (Comes over and takes the bottle out of my hand) And you don't even drink!

Me: (Leaning back against the bureau) Ah, but the lead character in the movie does. I have to get into character so I can write the damn script.

Helen sets the bottle down on the writing table.

Helen: (Taking a deep breath) Charlie, what's the problem?

Me: There is no problem.

Helen: The script is 3 days later. I would say that's a problem.

Me: No, starving children in Africa is a problem, Me not having a script done is an inconvenience.

Helen: An eighty million dollar movie is not an inconvenience! I need that script rethought, reword, revamped and refuckingwritten! We start shooting next week!

Me: You swear too much Helen. It's most unbecoming.

Helen sits down and stares at me with narrowed eyes. Neither of us speak for a good twenty seconds. The she tries a different approach.

Helen: Charlie, what's wrong? This isn't like you.

Me: (Picking a piece of lint off the front of my robe) I don't know. Maybe I just don't have anything to say anymore.

Helen: (In a soft town of voice) This script isn't about what you have to say. You don't have to say anything. All you have to do is spruce it up and make it workable.

Me: I can't. It just doesn't work.

Helen: All your scripts work! The last movie you wrote grossed over 200! You can do this Charlie!

Me: (Raising my voice) But this isn't my script Helen! The script was written by some kid in Kansas! This is HIS work, not mine!

Helen: That's my point! You don't even have to write, just edit!

Me: I'm not an editor, Helen. I'm a writer.

Helen: (Upset again) Then write the fucking thing!

I go over to the table and retrieve my bottle. I pour some whiskey into a coffee cup and put the bottle back down. I silently sip the drink as I sit back down on the bed.

Helen: (Lowering her voice) We've known each other a long time, haven't we?

I don't even bother to nod.

Helen: So you can talk to me Charlie. Just tell me what's going on and we can sort this out.

Me: I already told you, I don't have anything to say.

Helen: Alright. We've established that you have nothing to say. But can't you just hammer this script out?

Me: What's the point?

Helen: (Getting to her feet) The point? You have to ask what the point is? How about this: If you don't get that fucking script done you won't be working anymore! Dennison will fire you and if he gets rid of you nobody is going to pick you up! You'll be finished!

Me: (Lifting the cup in a toast) Que, cera, cera.

Helen: And I'll be fired too. Not that you would give a shit.

Me: Don't be melodramatic. You're indispensable.

Helen: You need more motivation? (She snaps her fingers at Jenny) Take your clothes off!

Jenny stares wide eyed at Helen.

Me: What are you doing Helen?

Helen: Motivating you. You need to get out of this funk. Maybe you need to get laid. (To Jenny) Go on, get undressed!

Jenny tentatively reaches a hand to the top button of her blouse.

Me: Jenny, stop.

Helen: Me then? (She pulls the tails of her blouse out from her skirt)

I stand up and go back to the bureau.

Me: Helen, stop that.

Helen: (Her blouse still not tucked in) So what is it? Are you depressed? Have you gone nuts?

Me: (Smiling) Anyone who doesn't want to sleep with you must be depressed or insane. You should really work on that low self esteem.

Helen: (Tucking her blouse back in) Then what Charlie? What is so bad that you can't write?

I rub my hands down my unshaven face.

Me: (Taking a deep breath) I already told you.

Helen: That you have nothing to say? (She picks up the script and shakes it) It's already been said! All you have to do is make it sound better! That's it!

Me: That's not it at all. You just don't understand.

Helen: (Pleading) Then make me understand!

I take a deep drink and set the cup down.

Me: I used to write novels you know.

Helen: I know that. I even read a few of them.

Me: Then you know that I wrote some beautiful things.

She nods. Jenny nods.

Me: I used to turn words into musical notes! I used to write some goddamn beautiful prose.

Helen: (Quietly) I know.

Me: Even when I started writing scripts, I changed my style so that what I had to say could be parlayed into film. Even that fucking hack writing...

Helen: It wasn't hack writing. It was great stuff. Hack writing doesn't get nominated for an Oscar.

Me: It IS hack writing! I wrote what some studio head told me to write! I wrote scripts because I couldn't write novels anymore! I needed italics and camera angles on the page! But even then, I tried to write it in my own voice so I could be heard. Helen, that's what a writer is. Someone who has something to say. Somebody who can turn thoughts into print, make an ethereal thought earthly and clear. It's making those words sing! (I look down at my hands) Now I can't even make someone speak without sticking a colon after their name.

Helen sits silently, looking down at her own hands.

Me: And what's left to be said? Is there a story out there that hasn't been told? How many times can we hear about boy meets girl, boy fools around with girl, boy and girl save the world? It's all tripe now and I can't even do that anymore.

Helen: (Standing up) What can I say to you?

Me: Nothing, absolutely nothing.

Cut to:

My shaking hands.

Me: I can't even write a short story without it turning into a hack script.

Helen: I think you should THIS script and then take a nice long vacation. Go out to the mountains or something and be a hermit. Find out what you've lost and figure out a way to get it back.

Me: (Quietly) But first finish the script.

Helen: Yes, first finish the script. Then once it's done you go away for a while. Maybe then you can write another novel.

Me: (In barely a whisper) But first finish the script.

Helen comes over to me and places her slender hand on my shoulder.

Helen: Will you do that Charlie? Will you finish the script?

I nod.

Helen: Will you? I want you to say it.

Me: I'll finish it.

Helen walks over to the far table and picks up her purse.

Helen: You can do it. I know you can. Charlie, no more bullshit, you're a great writer and you can do this.

Me: I'll do it.

Helen slings the purse over her shoulder and comes back to me. She kisses me on the cheek and then pats my back.

Helen: Damn right you can do it. I'll give you a call tomorrow.

Helen turns and walks to the door. Jenny hands Helen her coat and then opens the door for her. Helen walks out.

Jenny: (In a whisper) I really liked your last novel.

I smile.

Jenny exits and the door closes behind her. I can hear tow sets of high heel shoes clicking purposefully way.

Cut to:

A blank page.

Twenty First Century Sage

I love sex. That's why the sacrifice was so great.

I had been celibate for 5 years and 3 months and I picked the day of my best friend's funeral to put an end to my re-born virginity. The reasons behind any self-imposed period of chastity are always complex and mine were no different. I made the decision when I was younger and wiser and horribly idealistic. Though the decision was hard fought, the application of it was not difficult. I'm not rich or handsome and I'm not all that bright. It is true that availability dictates the level of temptation but celibacy is not abstinence, it goes beyond the denial of engaging in sexual acts. Celibacy expunges and yet replaces. It was my greatest desire to put away the lusts of the flesh, to seek out truth and to buffet away all the venality in me. The quest for higher wisdom was aflame in me but it was all borne of guilty. I was in love with an unapproachable woman, my best friend's wife. I loved her, in that one sided ideal – unrequited, unknown way that mortars fantasy. Those desires stayed with me for 5 years, always on the edge of my thoughts, along the borders of denial, between the margins of philosophy. I realize now, I had never become a celibate.

I hadn't seen my friend in all those years and when word reached me that he had drowned in Mexico, my first thoughts were all made of shame. I lusted after his wife, I coveted his very life and because of those wicked desires I had removed myself from him. Now we has dead and all the feelings that I bore for his wife were finally gone. She was now sacrosanct, beyond even my basest wishes. Through my friend's death, she had transformed into a grieving widow, a desperate mother of three young children and a paragon of virtue, because tragedy imparts virtue, like making heroes out of idiot children that fall into wells.

I attended the funeral and averted my eyes from all familiar faces. I stared at the coffin, at the priest, at the freshly turned soil. When all the prayers were muttered, I beat a hasty retreat and went straight to the nearest hotel. I went to the deserted lounge, took a seat at the bar and ordered a double rye and coke. My suit itched, the hand that held a cigarette trembled and my mouth remained parched, even after the bartender made three trips to my spot at the bar.

I hadn't had a drink in over 5 years. I hadn't smoked in over 5 years. I hadn't engaged in sexual congress in... as if on cue, a woman took a seat at the bar, two stools down from me. I quickly looked away as she took off her coat and I heard her order a Tom Collins. Through casual glances I took note of her long brown hair, her pale features, her figure. I wanted to devour her with my eyes but I kept cool, looking at the ashtray, then over to her face, her thin nose and the pale red of her lipstick. I focused on my drink, then her legs, clad in tight black slacks. I looked at the bartender, then the curve of her thigh as she crossed her legs. The TV tuned to Jeopardy, then her breasts. "What is the Hudson River?" Correct for 200 dollars. She wore a white sweater and at that moment I swore that if that sweater had been anything other than white, I would have walked away. But white is for purity and white is for innocence and white is for the soft flesh, rounded and silky, warm and begging to be... The Nile was the answer to the next question.

I was discreet. I flicked my eyes from her to the TV. She never caught me looking and as I turned my mind away from her, I actually tried to think which category I would choose next. The contestant chose "Explorers" and I got the first one right. "Magellan." I even said the answer out loud and earned a smile from the woman.

"Where are you from?" She asked and I felt my breath catch in my throat. It was the kind of question you ask in a hotel, when you're not from the city, when you're here on business or pleasure or looking to while away the minutes before dinner is served. Maybe it's a tourist thing to do.

My voice came out ragged, "I'm from here."

"How old are you?" She asked after a long stare. "I know it's rude to ask, but…"

I said, "Not at all…"

I smiled when I told the woman my age but was wise enough not to ask her in return. I guessed that she was around the same age as me and I allowed myself a closer look at her smile, at the crinkle in her nose. I looked back at the TV and she followed suit. She even answered the questions and got a few correct. I said something cute and she said something witty and after her second drink she was on the stool next to me and before Alex Trebek signed off, she bit her lip and looked me in the eyes. "I saw you staring at my tits."

I must confess, that word sealed my fate. "Tits." The word changed and became a dirty bit of song when that woman described a part of her anatomy the way a man would. Had she said breasts, I might have blushed and that would have been the end of it. And it was 5 years, and it was a host of bad reasons and that evening I didn't want to feel guilty or ashamed or remotely abstemious. I don't know what I said in return and I don't know what she replied but I left half a glass full of rye on top of the bar and followed her upstairs to the fourth floor.

I wanted to run to her room. Because as I said, I'm not rich or handsome even that smart, so it had to be fate that this woman wanted to be with me. I was operating under a higher power and was redeemed.

The room was dark and thankfully she didn't wait before she turned and kissed me. It was a hard, bruising kiss and it hurt my lips. I hadn't kissed anyone in… but it didn't matter because here was a woman who didn't even want to know my name or my thoughts on Sartre or if I'd ever read The Dharma Bums. My heart was pounding and my breath was ragged and the feel of my hands on her back and her waist might have been enough for her. Maybe she just wanted to feel young and unknowing, maybe we could be teenagers again and just neck and pet. I tried to remember the feel of a breast underneath a bra and if I could still unclasp it it with one hand. But the kiss turned a little sweeter and her lips were softer and her tongue tasted like a stolen candy. Her hands went to my chest and she gave a little push. As she moved away from me, the dim light cast shadows across her face and the velvet gloom cloaked her body.

I was sexual anxiety and ego run wild and I could almost stand back and watch as my conflicting wants dueled and danced in a thrust and parry ballroom before my eyes.

She turned on the light next to the bed and crooked her finger at me. I came over as gracefully as I could but I wanted to run, pounce, feed the bestial need. I tripped over her shoes. She giggled, I chuckled and then levity was banished, because her nipples were hard and thrust against her white (white is for what?) sweater and her lips were against mine and her hands were peeling off my jacket, undoing my shirt and tie. I lifted off her sweater and kissed her neck, her shoulder, the swell of her cleavage and her hard nipple was slick from my mouth. Naked from the waist up, we fell on the bed and as we kissed and touched and pulled away what was left of our clothes, my mind reviewed the checklist. The necessary rules of foreplay must be adhered to. I mentally ran down my to do list. Kiss her breasts, suck her nipples, I had to caress her ass... wait, what comes next? Isn't passion supposed to be mindless and instinct driven? "Of course not!" quoth my inner 16 year old. It's kissing, necking and maybe a bit of biting. It's touching, tasting, searching, exploring. Then it's oral sex. Who goes first? This wasn't a first date, this was a one night stand. This was primordial lust and there are no rules. I figured it out in time, because as my lips went past her belly button she growled, "Just fuck me."

Duel natures prevail with love and sex and in me, Narcissus was exorcised, going off to the bathroom to flex in front of the mirror and I was left with some kind of Woody Allen inside me, flushing anxiously. I closed my eyes for a second, almost cringing because I wasn't ready. I wasn't hard. I wasn't hard. I wasn't hard. Thank God, I'm hard.

She moaned when I entered her and she pushed against me, her pelvis rising. I let out a gasp, because half a decade has a way of making one forget. She was so wet and so hot and she could flex the muscles in her vaginal wall and for a second I tried to think, what are those things called? What's the name of that exercise? Kegels? Who cares? It was almost manipulative and not at all instinctual, but again, who cares? Maybe she had her own inner 16 year old.

As I moved faster she moaned louder and when she looked up at me, she had this weak smile and I felt grateful for that. She whispered something but I couldn't hear and she whispered again but I still didn't catch it then with a push she had me off her, on my back and she was on top. I think she did that because her hair was stuck underneath her. I think that was what she was whispering about. "Whet off my hair." I don't know.

But I forgot right away because she was pushing down mightily and I was thrusting up and she looked so damn sexy, riding me and staring down at me and her hands on my chest and…no, not yet, not yet you weak bastard! 5 years or not, you can't come yet! So I close my eyes because the sight of her on top of me is enough to make me come. I think about something other than fucking, like books or movies. But I AM fucking someone. Someone IS fucking me. I'm part of a fucking situation! I held it back, once, twice, and then, after a groan of pain, three times and then I realized that I wasn't wearing a condom. I hadn't bought a condom in… you know how long. She didn't seem to mind and I actually remember biting my lower lip in fear. I looked up at her face, her head thrown back, her back arched, her hips grinding, the smacking noise flesh on flesh and the creak of the bed and the way I was moving, the way I couldn't stop but coming was out of the question now. It was too late anyway. I was going to get some kind of disease. Then she did that thing again, gripping me insider her. Funny how a fear of disease or death falls away while in the throes of passion.

She let out a tiny, high pitch scream (who can tell with women? I mean, is any of it real?) She swiveled against me, crushing me, and then she fell forward, coming to rest against my chest. The weight of her, the feel of her sweaty skin... was heaven. I didn't think about cute after sex repartee or awkward silence. I thought about how I wanted to her my arms around her and run my fingers against her skin. I wanted to kiss her softly and hold her forever. This couldn't be a one night stand, because God damn it, I'm a moral and upright person! I'm a goddamn sage after all. I wanted to know her name and follow her home and make her breakfast every morning. I wanted to know that I wasted 5 years and that all my good intentions and acts of denial were made moot. Because this moment was good and true beautiful and I could start to live again! I could start to be alive! I could love and be loved and this achingly perfect moment could be the start of my, no, of OUR new life together.

She lifted her face from mine and smiled at me. I smiled back. She rolled over and sat on the edge of the bed, her back to me. I stoked the line of her spine and desire flushed through me again. Desire for her, for us. She turned to face me, "You better get dressed, my husband will be back soon."

I hate sex.

THE LIVING MYTH

With my back pressed against the wall, I counted out the steps, with my heel against my toe, one foot in front of the other. Exactly twelve steps. I hadn't done it before. Beside the bed, I measured from the back wall to the bars, seven steps, not quite exact. There is a small mirror on the wall and I smiled at the reflection, a menacing smile that looked good to me. I was always looked great in orange, and the jumpsuit suited me just fine.

There are no books on the shelf. Nietsche and Milton are no longer married, pressed against each other, cover to cover. They're happily divorced, as they should be, back in the library, filed a la Dewey. My bed is small, as you would expect, but neatly made. But there is no time for sleep. Time is pressing on, and that brings me back to the table. It's a small table, with a plate, a fork, a knife, all used. Sadly, it was not any kind of Amuse-Bouche, but the Portobello mushrooms, filet mignon, and crème brulet were a welcome change. Next to the plate is a letter from my wife, who had no idea, right up until the end. Barbara, my pale wasp wife thought I was an importer. I'm trying to think of something clever to say about a hired killer masquerading as an importer, but I'm drawing a blank. Maybe there's nothing clever about it.

On the table, next to the letter and the plate, is a yellow legal pad and a Mount Blanc pen. It's time to sit down again, before the man comes to do my portrait. Write, write, write away, but as I said, time presses on, so I cannot dot the I's or cross the T's. There will be no flowing script for me, just blocky print, and to the point.

Ask me about choice, as I sit in this cell awaiting the cry of angels. People talk about personal choice and accountability as if they were valid, as if they were real. They aren't. The infantile cry of the adolescent is gospel – I never asked to be born. It wasn't my choice. Both nature and nurture were beyond my control.

Predestination isn't a solid defense, either legally or spiritually. God, like the federal judges, has no sense of humor. In fact, neither do I. A fan of irony and a shameless abuser of sarcasm I may be, but my soul, or whatever that pit just under my seat of magnanimity is, is black and burnt. That sounds dangerously close to a confession and I have not been weak enough to succumb to that dreary acceptance of culpability. I committed the crimes, fine, it's done. It's too late to lie about it and admittance on its own can never be mistaken as repentance. Not in the Heavenly court, and not at Manhattan Federal.

Nevertheless, though I will not foist all the blame on myself, I have to accept some of it. Because upbringing and genetic predisposition aside, I became a killer out of boredom. I learned early on that all manner of conventional stimuli were fleeting, weak excuses for living. Pleasure is not happiness. And truthfully, (almost as a confession) I can say that killing certainly did alleviate the boredom. Killing did indeed make me happy.

But how did it make me happy? Why did it bring such joy to me? I won't prattle on about the answers because it is so bloody obvious. I was masquerading as God. How can music, food or sex replace that feeling? They cannot. It doesn't really matter though. The time to mount a defense is long past, so there's no point. I don't care to plumb the depths of my terrors or grabble with the reasons behind my boredom or my desire. I was paid to kill, I enjoyed it, so let the wherefore remain a mystery. People die all the time so really, where is the tragedy? If I hadn't come along, all those people that died by my hand would have met their end at some time. But it's not that simple is it? I loved it and I made a mistake. Obviously, otherwise I wouldn't be here writing about it.

It was my secret, my extra marital affair, and it was so monumentally delicious that I had to share it. There, that was my downfall. Sharing. The axiom of the playground was my undoing.

For the same reason that Mormons go door to door, I took a young zealot under my wing. I was a joyous proselyte and he a most hesitant but attentive disciple. He accepted my good news with a slavering restraint. Lord, how he resisted. He quailed and struggled, but he could not deny his needs. I was educated, rich and dare I say it, handsome as a devil but none of that impressed him. He was poor and ignorant and ugly, but the quality in me that he strove for was my black soul, my deft, evil heart.

I wish to God that I could paint a picture of this acolyte. His base evil was thickly cloaked in innocence. His brutal hands made fists in false, velvety gloves. His very essence was divine... but divinity through distorted glass, a fallen angel clinging to a high white cliff. Lucifer, on the brink of a name change. He wasn't scum or common street trash devoid of morality. He was moral! He was Stephen's twin, a martyr, but the stones I hurled blossomed bruises that he loved. He was an addict of evil, and that's what made him so wonderful. There was no gleeful murder in him; it was somber and halting, hesitant and pensive. It was beautiful. As a pair, what we did was art, because we complimented each other so very well. I was ruthless and he was full of pity. I was willful and he was obedient. I was lonely...

We lived with a glorious, passionate hatred that brimmed over from our souls. It set us apart from the huddled, frightened masses. It divided us, elevated us, set us on high, away from the dirty, plain people. My friend, my desperate, fading brother, was bound to me by oath and by choice. In my madness he joined me and swam the murky depths of depravity with me. My soul whispered that he would never leave me. Not for lucre would he betray me, not for love or pain or torture would he leave my side. God damn the man, he was Roland to my Charlemagne and I didn't deserve him. Even later, I didn't deserve his stare when I took the gift of hatred and turned its glare upon him.

I wish that I didn't have to disgrace my pure emotion with

comparisons to love, but some feel that the two go hand in hand and who am I to argue? Love, which is weak, fleeting, capricious and common. Any love, all love, is born from a rotten seed. A mother's love is selfish and petty, a warm strangulation made of arrogant need. A need to smother and protect, to glorify herself as a loving god. All the while, that child is denied the world and made into a suckling retard. Better to be a shark, and let the children swim. Better to be a reptile, and leave the brood to fight on the sand alone. A mother's love is a sick thing.

Then there is the despotic god Eros, the one who glorifies the vapid and the idiotic. Fat Cupid, Psyche's pimp, he makes fools and dotards of us. Watch two lovers and you'll see love in its most banal form. It's based on nothing, built on sand, temporary and temporal, it is only lust dressed up for a gala ball. True love! True love! I'll place a chocolate bar on your pedestal and no one will know the difference. The same endorphins will dance, fatuous and coated in a numbing vacuity. Eros is playfully cruel, he lives to watch us flail but I couldn't and wouldn't. Slavering Romeo and whorish Juliet, a dog at its master's feet displays a love more pure.

Still, Love cheated me, when I was blind. I loved my brother, my friend, my apprentice. He was nothing before me. He was stupid and weak and lost. He was young, and needed me. It's all truth, no word of a lie. You can believe me, because I know that without him, I was all those things and more. I needed him as well.

He rose and fell at my behest, he drank and smoked and cavorted when I told him to. He stole and fought and killed and he did it nobly, beautifully. He followed when I led, he charged at my command and then he sat behind a mahogany rail and pointed his finger at me. Faithless mutt, he turned rabid. God curse him, God destroy him, God turn Your vengeance upon him.

I used to want to go back, to erase the events of that last night but I know that given the chance, I wouldn't change a thing. It was no different than before. We wore the same mantle and our minds were set on things above. I was given no hint that he had changed.

Or maybe I had, but I wiped those thoughts away, so blind was my trust, so great was my affection for the damnable man.

It was a hot, smothering night when we left Dante's bar. My shirt clung to my sides and my hair stuck to my forehead. My shoes felt soft against the pavement and I walked silently, like a predator. Half a step behind, my friend spoke my name in a whisper.

I turned and saw him looking across the parking lot to a red Karmann Ghia parked all by itself. A young woman was fumbling in her purse for her keys and my friend was frowning.

She was the mistress to a powerful man, a secretive and important and public man and she had to go. She always waited in the car, no matter how hot it was outside. She waited like a dutiful wife, like a supplicant... like clockwork. My friend and I had done our homework, we'd watched and waited and our eyes were more piercing, seeing beyond her beauty. We knew that it faded by the second.

We kept walking so as not to attract attention to ourselves and when we got to my car we got in and stared out the passenger window at her. We argued that night. He wanted to stop, he wanted to quit and at first I berated him. I called him weak, I called him a coward, but he remained obstinate. I cooed and cajoled, building up his frothing hate. Finally I told him that it would be the last time, noting how easy it was for the lies to tumble out of my mouth. I never wanted it to end. I told him that I would do as he asked after one last hurrah. I would say anything to keep him. In the end he gave in, with a nod and a sigh. He stared at me and I wanted to hug him but instead I kept smiling. I knew that he wanted her dead too, but he was afraid. He was always afraid. It's why I loved him so! He was innocent, in the way that all great killers are.

We'd been there before, in different parking lots and alleyways and deserted streets and rooms. My friend had been strong and dependable. Even that night, that horrible night, he was true to form.

That night murder stank of sweat and leather. The leather seats, her coat, her purse, my shoes. And sweat... from three hot bodies, two killing, one dying. It was brutal and bloodless. My friend was a master with a garrote, a virtuoso when it came to strangulation. He was strong and quick and all I had to do was hold the woman down, so she couldn't thrash and maim. It was quick and her death melted into us, my friend and I. It oozed from her lungs in a dying gasp and entered us, numbed us, turned our hearts to a dingy gray. And it was easy. I took in deep breaths of stale, spirit filled air. No thoughts intruded then. Those came later. Even so, they were only pleasant musings on the bonds of living and dying and I lost myself in memories of the victim. I smacked my lips with the thrill of it, of her, of me, and of my friend. Till death do us join, amen.

I called, but my friend did not answer. I visited his home and some girl, some waif of a thing, told me that he had left. I smelled the lie on her. I waited for him to come to me, and when the police came instead, I swore a silent oath as they shackled me, swearing that betrayal could not have come from him. It was impossible. It was beyond any nightmare. He would never betray me. That was the mantra I chanted, that was the prayer. But I was fooling myself. Delusion never tasted so bitter.

The police had me in the interrogation room for seven hours and I never cracked. I never broke. Seven hours of threats, of promises, of rewards dangled on a stick. Seven hours of filthy cop stink, of stale coffee and dry cigarettes. Cigarettes that crumble when they're lit, cigarettes so dry that you can hear them burn. Seven hours of a cold steel chair and cold steel stares and smoke and bad breath and body odor. I never cracked. Seven straight hours, and it didn't make a difference. All my strength was made moot.

Soon after my friend was staring at me and I swore that I saw him smile and he was pointing his finger at me and the prosecutor was beaming and the judge was frowning and the jury was shocked and appalled and they hated me. But I hated them too. All of them, but mostly my friend, God damn him.

So he is free and I am chained and my confession (it IS a confession, poor me) is too late to bring justice or salvation and no one is justified, no one is redeemed. No one is free, only the dead and dying... and me too, I only now realize. My prayers are laced with cyanide, my meditations are made of knives, and my soul screams torture, revenge, black justice: that my friend, now free, feels the agony of the chasm that lies between us. I want him to suffer alone, adrift, cast away and cut off. His freedom haunts me, these last few moments before I die, and it isn't envy that I feel for him, but common hatred. Hatred is my gift to him. The gift we once shared. In the name of justice I will join the ranks of the gone and he is forced to march on, all alone. Justice has been rendered to us both. Both of us will be punished and as we lived so shall we die, connected by the blood we spilled and the blood that races through our hearts.

If by killing, I was made into God, then God is a coward. My limbs are heavy and the heavy steps of the priest come closer. My heart is pounding, my cheeks are damp with tears. There are no excuses, there are no pithy remarks left in me. I am friendless, loveless, and even without hate now. I am spent and empty. I am ready.

50 Minutes - 3 Voices from the Ward

ROOM 511

Sometimes things are hazy before medication

The rain began to come down in sheets, sending the partygoers running for the veranda. The girl, without letting go of my hand, stepped out in the downpour. Her long hair darkened and fell flat against her cheeks, "What would you say if I asked you to dance with me on the lawn?"

"I would say that you're mad." I smiled, "But that madness becomes you."

Then, arm in arm, we dashed out to the lawn and waltzed under a canopy of crying clouds.

The night ended with a kiss on her parent's porch. It was a different time, 1955.

Sitting across from me is a girl who looks like Heaven on a sunny day. Right now she's dipping her tea bag absentmindedly while reading a book. I wonder what kind of tea it is. I wonder what book she's reading. I wonder if she's ever been alone, or in love, or just lived life like an empty plastic bag blowing down a street on a windy day. Before all this is over, I'll be in love with her. Maybe, at the very least, I'll go over and introduce myself. I wonder if she knows who I am. I wonder if I should tell her.

I'm the hero. If there was ever any doubt, put it aside now, because I'm telling you the truth. This is my little story and I'm the hero. Ask anyone who knows and they'll tell you that people have to like the hero. He has to be good, brave and dashing. Either that or he has to be bad, reckless and sexy. Maybe he's got to be funny, or between 5'10 and 6'1. He has to have great hair and big muscles, or purposely bald and lean. He's got to do something amazing and life altering. He's got to be everything you're not. He's all the little hopes and dreams that you've hidden or acted out in front of a mirror. He's what you want. Or something like that. Something I'm not. But make no mistake... I'm the fucking hero here.

If you're wondering about that little italicized blurb at the top of the page, I'd better tell you that it came from Page One of my great novel. The novel to charm and enchant, with a hero and a heroine to put all others to shame. It would have been beautiful... it would have been art. It would have changed your meager life. I never wrote it. Six lines. That's it. The story I'm about to tell you is nowhere near as sublime as the novel would have been but it has something even better. It has the truth. Sure, you're rolling your eyes now, but maybe you'll be dabbing at them with a Kleenex before we're through.

Sometimes I'm in a different place

You could say it ended with that last line about how the world was a different place back in '55 and you'd be right. Everything ended there, because if I were given the grace to write three hundred more pages, I wouldn't be the man I am today. Graceless, hopeless and just plain less, but at least what I am is real and true. I no longer believe in fairy tales and true love and neither should you. Do you doubt me, skeptical reader? I hope you do, because your cynicism just proves my point. MY POINT: The world is shit and you are too. So, how do ya like me now?

The girl has just brushed her hair behind her ear for the tenth time in the last five minutes. It's such a simple gesture and it makes me tremble just to see her do it. That book she's reading must be good because she hasn't taken her eyes off it. Maybe if I let out a little cough to draw her attention. Maybe I should just lean forward and say, "Excuse me miss, but would you mind breaking my heart?"

I was ruined by a woman. Actually, she only set the wheels of destruction in motion. I don't want to bestow any undue credit upon her. I hate her, but she isn't to blame, as all heartless wenches are blameless, but she guided the hand of Fate and forced it into a fist. She curled Fate's gnarled knuckles over and then promised a blowjob in exchange for a pounding on her ex. By the way, Fate's real name is Mike. Mike (or Fate) works as a bouncer in a grimy club downtown. Mike is 6'2, 240 and runs the quarter mile in who the fuck cares. He's good looking enough to sell cigarettes and cologne on the back pages of Rolling Stone. He has perfect teeth, a great smile and is always sensitive to a woman's feelings right before he tells his buddies about her tits. He's a slack jawed, knuckle dragging urban hillbilly who hasn't read more than three sentences strung together at one

time and that includes the instructions on condom packages. And yeah, he beat the shit out of me at the behest of my ex. The two of us met up right after line five in the above italics. Line six was a desperate attempt at courage and forgiveness, but one line was all I had in me. Beatings like the one I got tend to give one the impression that life isn't all debutante balls and kisses in the rain.

In retrospect, I deserved it. I was an asshole, as hard as that may be to believe. I was an asshole in the way that all true assholes are. I loved someone. I gave up my pride, dignity and right to piss with the big dogs so I could be loved in return. If that isn't an asshole, I don't know what is.

Sometimes the nurse has to sedate me

Before you get impatient, this isn't a story about love and loss.   It isn't about boy meets girl, boy loses girl, boy saves the world, boy bangs girl in her parent's bed.   If there is any kind of formula here, it's about how boy loses girl and gains the awful knowledge about life.

It begins with a guy sitting in a cafe.   The guy is me and the cafe is what surrounds me right now. I may have faked you out till now by giving you the impression that I knew where this was going. The sad truth is, the story begins now and I have no idea where or how it ends. You would have to ask the girl in front of me.   You could ask the couple in the corner booth, they might know.   Then again, if anyone knows, it wouldn't be them.   The frothed milk sipping, chain smoking, pale as the day is long and sunless, cafe dwellers.   They sure as hell wouldn't know; they don't even know that the hippies that they're trying so hard to emulate are driving BMWs and plotting out RRSPs.   Maybe in between sips of specialty coffee they're silently contemplating the exact hour when they'll sell out, grow up and donate their tacky clothes so the next insipid generation won't go clogless.

Sometimes I spend my whole day wishing

The fact is, no one knows where the story ends. I, the architect of this waste of paper don't even know.   It's been twelve days since my public humiliation at the hands of Mike.   My black eyes are turning purple and my swollen lip is healthy enough to press against my cup of near boiling decaf.   Twelve days since the story about young love in the fifties has died.

The young guy who works the counter here in hip cafe world is reading a dog-eared copy of Plato's Republik. He keeps looking up at the three girls who are sitting across the room from him.   They aren't looking though, so he holds the book up higher so the title is easier to read from far away. The book is probably in rough shape from him carrying it from one posing station to another.   It's obvious that he doesn't understand a word of it but I'm sure he thinks he looks brainy sitting there waiting for customers and reading a philosophy book.   Trust me sonny, I've read it, and it won't jive with your frayed bell-bottom desperation.   Read Ginsberg, Cassady or some other beat poet fuck up. Maybe that will make the girls come running. I wonder if I should tell him just that but he would only act shocked at my observation. Then he would launch into a misconstrued tirade on the three-fold nature of man. I know all that not because I'm observant or even because I'm judgmental. I know because I've done the same things that he's doing.

One of the girls at the table is actually looking now. She stands up and walks over to his table. "Holy shit," he thinks, "My time has come." Sorry partner, she just wants a refill and a chance to show off her belly button ring and rose tattoo. Nice. Aren't you daring!   You pierced yourself and paid the tattoo guy an extra twenty to scar a minor.   I want to give her my brightest and cheeriest sneer to let her know that I'm in the same clique. I have tattoos, darling. I have three silver rings hanging from my ear lobe and my pants are falling off my hips. Please buy it hook, line and stinker.

Sometimes I have to pretend

I'm one of you! I listen to Beck and Kurt Cobain was my god! I hate all jocks and preps and even though Goths are ugly, they kick ass! I was picked on and ostracized! I spent my high school years in the library reading about the medical benefits of hemp and wishing that the revolution would come before sixth period! I'm just like you!

I could do it you know. I could con that girl right in front of the lovelorn counter guy. I have this safe gay man charm that will get me brushing her hair on her quilted flower comforter. In fact, that's precisely what I would have done before the beating and my failed attempt at therapy in the form of a novel.

She walks past me, giving her upper lip a self-satisfied curl as her eyes sweep down on me like pennies falling out of an ivory tower.   Must be the black eyes and bruises. A true beatnik cafe loiterer doesn't fight, and those brown-eyed judgements tell me just that. Well fuck you, you phony. I didn't fight, I got a beating. There's a big difference. And what if I got these bruises from ramming my rubber Greenpeace dinghy into an oil tanker? I bet you'd like me fine then wouldn't you?

Yeah, I could con her but I can't con myself. I let her have her sneer back with change to spare. Who cares what she thinks? Who cares what any of these corduroy clad hypocrites think? One is ten and a mass execution of this lot would only hurt indie record sales.

Sometimes I realize what I am

I'm about ready to pack up and go back home but that girl is still reading and she's still the most beautiful creature I've ever seen. My coffee tastes bitter no matter how much sugar I pour in and I'm down to the last three cigarettes in my pack but she's still there. I'll light up one more and see if I can finish this off. I suppose you're getting pretty tired of waiting for a point.

I suppose I never loved my ex otherwise I couldn't hate her now the way I do. The truth is she made me love myself. She made me want her to satisfy my own love. I loved myself so much that I can't even speak her name without getting a pain in my chest. My chest, my stomach, my groin... they all ache when I think about how I sold out my integrity and manhood. I eviscerated myself on an altar made of false promises and Tuesday night movies. She robbed me of the only gift that I could ever give and it doesn't matter that I've walked through puddles deeper than her because she was profound enough to know what she was doing to me.

I'm bitter and I'm tired, and as much as the pain of loss and humiliation kicks me in the balls, what hurts the most is knowing the truth. I know how pathetic I am. I know how empty I've become. I had pain but there's nothing singular in that. We all have pain. We get it, we deal with it, we move on. At least, that's what we're supposed to do.

When she was gone I ate and drank pain. The strange thing about pain is that it can be so beautiful. It can make you reach a part of your soul that holds music. It can make your suffering into a wondrous piece of art. Haven't you been at your most pure, your most sublime, your most alive, when you're in pain? If you're face down in a pillow crying or staring into a mirror you see just how beautiful you are.

But that beauty can't last. We can't fall in love with it because we would cling to that thing that makes us beautiful and all we would have is a two-dimensional painting. The most incredible painting ever, but it wouldn't be real. We can't keep plastering perfume over the stink. It's in healing that we take a chunk of that raw beauty and use it as a building block. We build on that one piece and add all the other things that make us human. Then, and only then do we have the chance to be complete.

Sometimes I think I can get better

I'm taking a deep breath and ready to take my chance. I'm throwing caution to the wind and I'm really going to ask that girl across from me to dance, sing, laugh, and ruin me all over again.

What was it that I said? Without healing, we can never be whole? That's why I'm mad and bitter and so fucking empty. Because I couldn't heal. I couldn't get beyond line six. I couldn't go on and now here I am, with the cigarette burned down to the filter. Waiting and wishing for all the great things to materialize in front of me. I'm going to write this last line and then I'll push my chair back along with my luck. I'm now waiting and wishing for line seven.

I haven't completely lost my grip on reality. I'm on suicide watch and my parents are coming to visit me in an hour and the nurse is at her station and the doctor is in his office. I know that I'm not in a café and there isn't a girl waiting for me to fall in love again. I'm going to take the pills they're offering and I'm going to go on living.

ROOM 317

The chick across from me is brushing her hair and I'm staring at her like she's the biggest tart to ever lift a skirt. We're in the dorm, room 317, three floors and fifteen blocks away from the nearest nightclub and she's getting all dolled up for a night of Friday night therapy and medication. These chicks are the dumbest and sluttiest trailer trash whores that I've ever come across. And that's saying a lot.

Nicole, the big assed fifteen year old says her old man used to visit her as soon as wifey was asleep. She tried to slit her wrists three weeks ago and ended up here. What is it about chicks and slitting their wrists? It's like, fuck thirty years of feminism. We're all supposed to be doing our part in trying to end stereotypes and here's some fucked up fifteen year old with her Lady Bic, hell bent on keeping us on the pussy side of suicide.

Sitting on the cot next to me is Marsha who claims to be a nymphomaniac. I told her that she was nothing but a slut and she cried, saying that she got no pleasure out of sex. It was a compulsion. I told her it was a compulsion for me to tell the truth. Stupid cow, she was going down on her seventeen-year-old cousin when she was twelve and upon hearing that, I knew that I had to be here for all the wrong reasons.

All these chicks are in here because of sex. Once again, it's nice to know that the hard fought victories of Andrea Dworkin and Catharine MacKinnon are going down the tubes because these psycho sluts have nothing but dicks on their minds. I swear it's enough to make Gloria Steinem turn over in her sitz bath.

Ok, enough about my bunkmates. This isn't about them. It's about me.

I'm not in here because of sex. I'm not in here because of incest, rape or cellulite thighs. I'm not a seventeen-year-old virgin either, so you can forget about that being an issue. I'm not even in the fucking dorm, because they won't let me sleep next to the other cooze. No matter, I'm in here just like they're in here. We don't have to share a room to share a sentence. They're in for sex and I'm in here because... well, I've yet to figure out the wherefore, but like that matters. I'm here and that's that. Just like before I came here I was in another place and before that somewhere else. The setting changes but nothing else does. Isn't that the sad truth?

I was born and raised in Littleshittown, in the state of Anywhere, in the grand country of Next Door To You. Actually, it was a small town, with one street that they called Main. There was one clothing store for men and another for women. One barbershop and one beauty salon. One school. Two churches.

I got out before I fell in love with a farm boy and traded in my sanity. I went to live with my sister in the city. My sister Eileen is twenty-two years old and three years ago she was attacked while coming home from work. She went blind because some upstanding citizen stuck his exacto knife in her eyes. He was arrested three days later, went to court a month after that and was sentenced to ten years in the pen. He was paroled two weeks ago.

Eileen is the prettiest girl I have ever seen. She is tall and slim with long auburn hair and the greenest eyes. Her boyfriend Trevor is cute too and he was really nice at first. Every weekend they rented movies and they curled up on the couch, munching popcorn and holding each other.

Trevor would describe what was going on in the movie while Eileen asked questions like, "Did the bomb just go off?" "What's she wearing?" "Is he crying?" Trevor always told her exactly what was going on. He didn't even need to watch the movie; that's how good of a storyteller he is. He could just sit there and hold Eileen and tell her the greatest stories.

I only stayed with Eileen for two months because things got weird. I would wake up in the middle of the night and feel hands all over me, tearing at me and dragging me off the bed. I'd wake up screaming and naked. This happened every night for three weeks and my sister was getting freaked. She wanted me to get help. Professional help. Fuck that, I said. I left. Trevor helped me pack. He wished me well with a hand on my ass. Fucking men, they all turn out that way. Even nice guys like Trevor.

I moved into one of those furnished fleabag hotels for seventy-five bucks a week. I was waiting tables at the time so my tips covered rent. I figured I would save up some cash and maybe start taking those night classes at the community college to get my diploma. I'd quit school a few weeks shy of graduation. Don't ask me why. Never ask me why I do anything I do. I do whatever comes to mind and it was in my mind that I had to get out of that tiny fucking town with its tiny fucking minds.

I slept OK those first few weeks. I never had one dream until I started school.

I thought my teacher, Mr. Desmin, was the greatest man I ever met. He was forty years old who looked like Richard Chamberlain. Minus the priestly frock, he was a shoe in for The Thorn Birds. I could tell you about how interesting he made his classes, or regale you with his convictions, warm your heart about how much he loved his children or inspire you with his genuine affection for his students. You wouldn't believe me because right after I told you all those fantastic things I'd have to mention that we started sleeping together.

So yeah, he was this great teacher who was banging his student after class. That blows all the good away doesn't it? His wife thought so too. When she gave him the ultimatum he chose her. She was the mother of his children and a ton of other things that I wasn't. What was I? Still firm where it counts and soft in the others. A young nymph who would go down on him under his desk while he corrected midterms. That's never enough to keep someone.

What did I care about rejection? Dick all. The problem was that the dreams came back. The worse the dreams became, the more I began to hate Mr. Desmin. He used me and then got rid of me, just like everyone else. It never mattered what I wanted to do. My happiness was moot.   Just like back home, when they wouldn't let me wear my skirts to school or shower with the other girls. Things could have been easy but there was always someone saying no to me. Not Mrs. Desmin, she was only staking her claim. It was that fuck Mr. Desmin who said no to me.

I planned to kill the motherfucker. I shouldn't say planned. I just decided to do it.   There was no planning involved.   I just waited around the school until he left and I caught him in the parking lot. I was a lot stronger than he was. What a pathetic speck he was. I stabbed him seventeen times. The same number of times that I let him mount me.

I thought about killing his wife, but we're sisters, deep down. As much as I hate to admit it, those trashy chicks in 317 are my sisters too.   All the cronies and young tarts back in the one horse town are also my sisters. No matter what anyone says.

I was going to go back to Eileen's place and take out the last vestiges of rage out on Trevor, but the cops got me before that. A blood-spattered dress tends to attract attention on a bus. If I had been smarter I could have got Mr. Desmin, Trevor, my father, my old school principal and all the other men who have fucked me one way or the other.

But don't get me wrong, I don't hate men. How could I? After all, I am one.

On the outside, I'm all man. But the outside never matters. But I guess the inside doesn't matter much either. Inside this blouse is a chest that grows hair. Under this skirt is a penis. Deep below my mascara, blush and lipstick is a face that needs a shave every day. Beneath the wig is a mind, a man's mind, full of violence and pain.

All my sisters in here are in because of sex and I guess, as tedious as it is to admit it, I suppose I am too.

ROOM 202

I'm here because I'm invisible, because I've spent my life unnoticed. I was like a movie extra: background on film, background in life. I lived by the rules and was thus able to blend in, slowly fade, and shuffle along until I vanished.

The rules don't apply to me now, because on the left side of reality is a cliché that curses, a kind of slogan for survival that sings itself over and over, "Greatness courts failure, greatness courts failure, greatness courts failure." The courtship is over. Greatness was a coy girl, batting her eyes and inching up her skirt. Failure is a sailor, battling the winds and doing deeds of courage. The two meet in a steamy port and Greatness tries to retain her virtue but Failure is a brute. On a bed of nine to five he rapes her and she becomes a harlot. She is given a new name and a new song. Now the boys call her Average and she piles the make up on thick to fool them.

Failure raped greatness and she bore him a son.

I'd tell people all the good things that I thought about them. I would tell every woman that she was beautiful and I'd tell her often enough for her to start believing it. I'd stop fat people on the street and tell them that I loved them. I would kiss every acne face and hug every droopy shoulder. I'd make the reject losers of the world lift their chins and feel proud. I'd make sure that the pretty girls focused on the inside. I'd tell them that they should be beautiful on the inside. I would take the dumbest person and teach them something. I'd knock the arrogant down a peg or two and then give them a hand back up. I want to do so many things.

Sometimes the crazy people who mumble and stumble in white hospital frocks are the freest. They're nuts. They have no responsibilities. They can shout as loud as they want. They don't have to worry what other people think or get embarrassed or uptight or nervous. They can be insane and liberated. I wish I could be liberated without going insane.

I hate the doctor who comes in to see me every Tuesday. Dr. Roger Shanus, arrogant prick and former Magna Cum Laude. He wears virgin wool vests under Harris Tweed sport coats. He smokes a pipe. His hair is greying at the temples. I hate him. I hate him. I hate him.

My parents came to see me yesterday. They came to visit. My dad didn't say a word. They stayed twenty minutes.

This is the end of all things, right in front of me. If they let their guard down, I'll be gone. I swear by all that is good and holy, Ill leave this place. They can't stop me because time is on my side. I can wait but they can't. That's why they send in the doctor and the nurses with little paper cups of water and pills. They don't leave me alone because they're impatient. They want me normal and functioning right away. Too bad for them, because they didn't figure out that I'm not the one that's sick.

Oh, all us crazy people think we're normal. We're the ones that see and understand. It's the rest of you that are blind, anesthetized and hopeless. Why do you think some of us scream? We've seen the horror of truth. We've seen mysteries unwrapped and secrets written in bold ink. We know what we're doing and I think I'm going to scream along with the rest of them.

I asked the nurse for a pen. I told her that I want to write my friends a letter. I asked for a nice red ink Sharpie, just for the symbolism. I'm writing this letter to you and then when I'm done I'm going to take that pen...

I've been out of the suicide watch room for two weeks now. That's why I'm here in the first place. I tried to fly. I stood on the rail of the High Level Bridge and was all ready for the big test flight when a car pulled over and a guy rushed over. "Hey buddy, hey buddy." I remember he called me buddy about fifty times. I got down off the railing, chicken-shit that I am. But not now.

Now they leave me alone. Stepping off that rail meant that I wasn't really ready to do it. I changed my outlook, thanks to the miracle of modern psychology. I think so and so does the doctor. Only what he thinks and what I think are two very different things. He says, "It's night, the sky is black." and I say, "It's night, the sky is red." Both of us are right, but one of us is more right than the other.

The night watch nurse has gone to her station way at the end of the hall and I have all the time in the world. When I'm done writing you I'm going to stab this pen into my throat enough times to open a big wound. I'll shove the pillow into my mouth so I don't make a sound. I can do it. All I have to do is lie quietly and wait. By morning, the nurse will find a nice bloody bed and one left behind body. I can do it. She'll be traumatized and I feel bad about that, but she knew the risks when she took this job and maybe it'll help her wake up. Her name is Carol. She's very pretty.

I know I can do it.

I'm 15 years old.

Green Sky Flood

Part II

I am a single mother. No, I have to remind myself, I WAS a single mother. First I was a mother, then a single mother, now I'm just single.

John, my late husband, used to be a kook, a crank, a nut, one of the crazies, because he believed that the government was evil and were plotting against the people. He moved us out of the city and we came here, to a small town. I didn't mind the move because I was born on a farm and I hated the city so the move was to my liking.

He insisted on erecting wind turbines and solar panels. I didn't mind that either because I believed it was good for the environment. John bought a ton of canned goods and a water purification system and I thought that was prudent, because as a child I had lived through a tornado and my parents and I were cut off from the rest of the world for 3 whole days, stuck in the storm cellar.

He used to get angry at the government, at the rich and the elite and accused them of wanting to starve us, enslave us, and kill us. I hated that because I believed that the government was nothing more than a group of people and people are essentially good. I was going to divorce him because I couldn't stand him being angry all the time. I didn't want him to impart all that hatred into our son. I was going to leave him but he left me, a week after the bombs dropped.

We lived far from "the target cities." When the bombs fell, John was almost happy, like he was proved right after all. He'd been telling me about secret bunkers in Colorado, about huge underground cities all prepared for the elite to live in once the outside world became unlivable. He showed me pictures and read me articles and gave me proof after proof but I was still going to divorce him and take our son away. It started with bombs and millions of people died. Then it was radiation and chemicals and billions died. John was dead in a week. He died in his sleep and he looked peaceful. I had to bury him myself.

A week later, our son died. He was only two years old and I buried him too. The neighbors, one after another... but I couldn't bury all of them so I buried none of them. I cough up blood and my hair has fallen out. I walk through town but there is no one left. Not one person. There are no dogs or cats or birds. I guess the smarty pants in their underground cities have zoos. I hope they do, I don't like to think about dogs and cats and birds all being extinct. I hope they have a regular Noah's Ark down there somewhere.

I don't go through town anymore because its emptiness will drive me insane. I strap on the pair of rollerblades that John bought me for my birthday and skate around the block. I stay in my own neighborhood because it still looks normal. The houses are intact, they're just quiet and still. I skate with my headphones on because I don't like the silence.

There's nothing on the TV except static. I have a huge collection of DVDs and box sets so I watch reruns of Friends and 90210 and Grey's Anatomy. I have a lot of movies too. Romantic comedies are my favorites. I stay away from action and drama and science fiction. I used to like them but not anymore. I threw all of John's stuff away.

The internet shut down a couple days after the blasts but I still play Solitaire and Tetris on the computer. I've re-read all the novels that I used to love. I eat soup and vegetables, picking the ones I like from the mountain of cans in the cellar. I heat them up in pots and eat them out of bowls. I do dishes every night. I make a pot of tea at night and drink coffee with whitener in the mornings.

And every day Willie comes by and it's a shame that he doesn't like to talk. If I went looking, I'm sure I would find more ghosts. There must be a lot of them because billions of people died and Heaven must be full. So they stay here and some of them come to visit me and draw pictures on my patio.

Waking Hours

What if…

Doesn't every great human undertaking begin with that query? What if we could reach China by sailing west? What if we could split the atom? What if man could walk on the moon? What if I could teach you to make your dreams come true this very night?

I mean it. All your dreams, all your hopes, all those fantasies and whimsical daydreams could be reality by tonight. When you close your eyes the dream tendrils that tickle you would be real. You would be there, leading the charge, winning the prize, getting the girl (or guy).

Think of that bully in school and now think of him getting his just rewards. Did your high school crush ignore you? Marry her tonight! Did your boss fire you? Fire him instead! Anyone who wronged you would be punished. Any goal you had would be achieved. The highest peaks would be scaled, the greatest depths explored and any kind of joy, happiness and pleasure would be yours.

Were you not strong enough, fast enough, smart enough? Tonight you are, and more. Are you alone? You don't have to be. Were you abused? That can disappear. Do you feel unloved? You can create all the love in the world and it can all be yours. It can happen…tonight.

Just imagine for a moment and play the "what if" game with me. This is how it would work: You would fall asleep and anything you wanted to happen in your dream would occur, played out right there in front of you. I'm not talking about those disjointed, vague and weird dreams that you have now. These dreams would be real!

You would wake up and your heart would be pounding because of the thrill, experience, because you were actually there. You fall asleep and right there in front of you is a huge drive in theatre screen and its playing out in full color, 3D, stereo sound and sharp as life detail. All you have to do is walk in…you're the star. The only limit is your imagination. You could have that every single night. Don't you get it yet, this is a place where you are God. You are God, without God's responsibilities.

There's a catch though. Nothing comes without a price, after all. There's life, with all its pain and disappointment and boredom and then there's…this other life. What price would you pay to be God of your own universe? Would you be willing to pay anything? Would you trade your own life?

I did.

***

I tried to be inconspicuous as I looked through the large window to Dr. Storvik's office. The old doctor was seated at his cluttered desk, leaning forward on his elbows as he listened to his two guests. Government folks, he nebulously called them in answer to my questions. As for what they wanted, that question went unanswered.

One of two intruders was a man in his forties, declared a bureaucrat by his simple black suit and pursed lips. The younger woman who sat beside him was a different story and it was because of her that I lingered by the window, absorbing every detail.

She was beautiful; it must be noted without hesitation. Her black hair was short, stylish and gleamed with health. Her skin was pale, but not sickly like mine. Hers was the color ivory, with a milky texture, again contrasting my own scarred features. She was tall and even when seated she appeared to be statuesque. Slim yet shapely, dressed in a pleated skirt and white blouse, she was the antithesis of her partner, who did none of the talking and all the scowling.

"Charlie, you're five minutes late for the interview."

I mumbled a reply to Lucille, the doctor's secretary, but I kept my eyes fixed on the woman inside. She was speaking and although I couldn't hear, I imagined her voice to be melodious and soft. Her hands moved as she spoke and each gesture was a minor ballet. Without warning she stopped and turned toward the window.

I took a step back, the glass showing my own startled reflection. Lucille's voice was sterner, "Charlie, they're waiting!"

I turned from the window, breaking away from the numb sensations that enveloped my body, the precursors to dream programming. I snapped my fingers at my sides to break the transition and left the outer reception area, my right leg even weaker than usual and dragging a little behind.

The hallway leading towards the interview room was long and tiled, bare of décor and painted a sterile white. My passage down that hallway was always declared by the sound of my footsteps. The sharp click of my left foot and the dull scrape of my right, a short shuffle that sent the tails of my white lab coat fluttering. The doctor liked to call it a dance but it was, in reality, nothing more than a lurch.

The main corridor always seemed deserted. The professional staff, which consisted of the doctor and two researchers, were barely enough of a presence. Then there was the indispensable Lucille, the support staff, kitchen workers and security guards that roamed the halls at odd intervals.

The facility was large, with a cafeteria, a lounge for the employees and the three offices, for Dr. Storvik, Phillip and Mary, the researchers. I lived in the nearly vacant west wing, along with the doctor, whose own spacious accommodations were two hallways down from mine.

Two separate dorms in the east wing housed the subjects who were involved in the program. Out of the thirty-two subjects, sixteen were inmates from a medium security prison, twelve were street people, looking for free room and board, and four were students who came in on a part time basis, making some tuition money.

I stopped in front of Examination Room B and took the clipboard that was affixed to the door. Clamped in place was the file belonging to Subject 24, Donald Blattner. I opened the manila folder and made a cursory glance down the last page to check notes that the other counsellors had made. Philip and Mary handled the medical research – the MRI's and Cat scans, the blood work and their corresponding data. I noted that Donald's latest medical data was not in the file, but that in itself was not unusual since Dr. Storvik often reviewed the subject's files independently. I opened the door and stepped inside the tiny room.

Seated in one of the chairs facing the table was Donald. He was a large man in his late thirties with colourful tattoos covering his thick forearms. His dark hair was graying at the temples and his face was creased with lines that appeared only when he smiled. I found it odd that a man convicted of double murder should have such affable wrinkles. He was smoking a cigarette and a quick look at the ashtray showed that he had been waiting longer than five minutes.

"Damn Charlie, you took your time today." Donald grinned as he spoke and I knew he wasn't upset by my tardiness.

"Sorry Donald," I said as I sat down opposite him.

He waved his hand in dismissal, sending a cloud of smoke my way. "I'm used to waiting around." He took a heavy drag from his cigarette and blew it away from me. "You ever been on the inside Charlie?"

I shook my head. "Came close a few times."

"You get used to waiting around in the joint"

I nodded. "I've heard that from the other inmates. They say the worst thing about prison is boredom."

"Damn straight, kid." He grinned, "Maybe if we had the dope you guys are giving out it wouldn't be so bad."

I uncapped my pen and grinned. "Ok, now we're back on topic. How are the dreams coming along?"

He leaned back in his chair with his hands clasped behind his head. "Unbelievable!" He winked, "I haven't had this many wet dreams since I was fourteen."

It was hard not to return his infectious smile but I almost managed. "Last week I wanted you to experiment with something beyond the erotic. You said you would work on something more detailed."

"Believe me Charlie, my centerfold dreams are pretty detailed."

I let out a exasperated sigh, "Donald…"

He laughed. "I'm just kidding around. I tried some of your suggestions."

"Which ones?"

"Oh, the boring travelogue dreams. Going to Paris, walking through the…what was that museum?"

"The Louvre."

"Yeah, the Loo-ver."

"And did you see the paintings from the book I gave you?"

He nodded. "Yeah, I saw em, but I gotta tell you Charlie, Playboy has got those dead guys beat for art."

I made some notes. "So, on a reality level, the dreams were high?"

He nodded slowly. "As real as you and I right now. But it's freaky. I wake up and I don't know where the hell I am. One minute I'm climbing a mountain, and then boom! I'm in bed wondering what the fuck just happened."

I put the pen down. "It takes some getting used to. Try to wind the dreams down at certain intervals. I don't want you waking up with a heart attack."

He thumped his chest. "Don't worry about my ticker. I'm not planning on dyin' anytime soon."

I smiled. "Now, has there been any problems programming the dreams?"

"You mean thinking up stuff I want to dream about? Hell no! I've got a vivid imagination!"

"Well," I said. "It says here on the dream log that you went a couple of nights without dreaming. What happened?"

He shrugged. "I dunno. I took the dope and fell asleep. Nothing happened."

I was silent for a moment or two. "Did you take the drug without programming? Because if you take it and sit in a dark room, you're probably going to dream about a dark room." He looked me blankly and I tried a different tack. "Ok, you take the medication and watch the evening news. What do you think you're going to dream about?"

"The stuff they showed on the news."

"Exactly. The dope…" I paused and shook my head. The *medication* opens your mind, makes it possible for you to feed information right into your subconscious. Do you follow?"

He nodded. "I get you. It's just that those two nights I was too tired to think about what I wanted to dream about."

"It only takes about five minutes…"

He cut me off, "I know, I know!"

I took out a sheaf of paper and handed it to him, "I've made a list of dream scenarios that I want you to enact. Take your time with the programming and try to get through all of them."

He scanned down the list. "Hmph, no bimbos in leather I see."

I laughed. "You can fit those in during your afternoon naps."

His face became solemn and he leaned forward. "You know Charlie, I want to thank you. All of you guys. This program saved my life. I had nightmares about them all the time."

"Them" referred to his victims, murdered over fifteen years ago.

I smiled but before I could say anything he kept on. "And having these dreams, they're better than life Charlie. They're better than anything that's ever happened to me."

I nodded. "I know, we're all pretty excited about the research."

"But this drug I'm taking. I mean, shit, something that good has to be bad for you. If there's one thing I've learned, it's that if something is too good to be true, then it probably isn't. You get me?"

My tone was harsher than I intended. "We've been over this Donald."

"Yeah, I know. And don't get me wrong, I'm about as grateful as anyone can be. Hell, even if it was killing me, I wouldn't stop. My dreams are better than my life... my dreams are my life now." He leaned forward and his eyes took on a wild look, "Me and the guys were talking about it and they agree. Unless you're a movie star or something, your life can't measure up to what we're doing. And think about it, an average person's day is broken up like this: 8 hours asleep. Probably about 10 hours a day for work if you factor in the time it takes to get ready, time spent in traffic, etc. That leaves 6 hours a day for things like making meals, eating, doing laundry, watching TV. Just imagine if you could drink a couple protein shakes and sleep for 20 hours a day, but during those 20 hours you're a spy or a world class athlete or whatever." His voice rose a notch as he got more excited. "Sure I dream about women a lot, but I also dream about going to the bottom of the ocean or flying through the clouds or being a wolf, chasing a deer through a forest!"

I smiled thinly and changed direction. "Tell me about the shape shifting dream. That one was pretty complex."

As Donald spoke about being a wolf, I could feel the beginning of a migraine. My hand started to tingle, a sharp pain began to creep up my back to my neck and a slow throb began at my temples. I had been experiencing the painful headaches for almost two months. They occurred every three or four weeks and increased in intensity with each attack. Dr. Storvik had given me some painkillers to take and they worked quickly and thoroughly but they also counteracted the pills that I took before bed. Dr. Storvik assured me that he was working on a solution to not only the medication, but the migraines as well.

The pain forced me to bite my lip and my right hand was shaking noticeably. Donald's voice became a dull mumble but I didn't want to take the pills in front of him. Being the prime guinea pig in the lab meant that any weakness in my condition was not to be known by the other subjects.

Donald noticed my discomfort and asked if anything was wrong. I quickly shook my head as I stood up and with a wane attempt at a smile I said, "I just have to go to the bathroom."

I picked up the clipboard and quickly left the room, closing the door behind me. Halfway down the hall was a water fountain and I quickly made my way over to it. I reached into my pocket and took out the bottle of pills, unscrewing the cap and popping the pill into my mouth before stooping to drink.

I drank heavily and took deep breaths, steadying myself against the water fountain. Black motes spun in front of my eyes as the pain reached its crescendo. I heard footsteps approach like dull echoes and I struggled to straighten up and to maintain my composure. I took a deep breath and turned toward the sounds.

Dr. Stovik and the woman were approaching. When they were a few feet away the doctor had a look of concern on his face but the woman remained impassive. "Are you all right Charlie?" The doctor asked in his mysterious European accent.

I smiled as best as I could, conscious of the pain but even more painfully aware that my hideous smile was being seen by the most beautiful woman I had ever laid eyes on.

"I'm fine, just a touch of vertigo. I didn't have breakfast."

The doctor wasn't fooled but the woman didn't show the slightest interest. She merely waited for the doctor to introduce her.

"You ought to know better, after a long night of research." Dr. Storvik smiled his fatherly smile and then turned to the woman, "Madeline Hearst, this is Charlie Graves. Charlie, Miss Hearst."

I bowed slightly and she nodded to me.

Dr. Storvik said, "Charlie, Miss Hearst would like to ask you some questions. Are you free at the moment?"

I reluctantly looked away from Madeline and addressed the doctor, "No, actually. I'm interviewing Donald."

The doctor gave me a disapproving look, "I'm sure we can reschedule Subject 24." Dr. Storvik never used the subject's proper names. He extended his hand toward another interviewing room, "Will this do?"

Madeline smiled thinly. "It'll be fine."

She entered the room and I cast a furtive glance down the hall, in the general direction of my room. I wanted to run to the safety of its four walls. My hand went to the doorknob but before I followed her inside, I looked back to the doctor with pleading eyes. He silently mouthed "It's OK."

She was already seated when I entered the room, feeling self-conscious of my limp as I clumsily made my way around the table to seat myself opposite her. I held the clipboard close to my chest and tried to fight the nervousness that threatened to bring the migraine back to its level of intensity. She opened the briefcase that she had set down beside her and took out a blank note pad and a gold pen.

Following these was a manila file folder similar to the one that was held in my clipboard.

She opened the folder and scanned its pages. After a minute of silence she finally looked up at me, her blue eyes unnervingly piercing. "Charlie Graves."

My own name sounded strange coming from those perfect lips. I simply nodded, not trusting my shaky voice.

"And you've been her for..." Her eyes swept down the page in front of her. "9 years?"

I nodded again.

"You were the first."

I bit my lower lip, nodding.

She stared at me for a moment and then her eyes softened. "You can relax Charlie, I'm not going to bite you."

I smiled without parting my lips and nodded again.

She paused, scanning the file again. Without lifting her head, she levelled her eyes at me with a smile and let out a small sigh. She closed the file, "Why don't you tell me in your own words how you came to be here."

I took a breath, "Could I ask you a question Miss Hearst?"

She tilted her head a little to the side and waited.

My voice cracked, sounding more shrill than usual. "Um, who are you and why am I being questioned?"

Her face seemed to harden again. "This project is Government funded, correct?"

I nodded, "Yes, but..."

"And that would make you answerable to the Government."

"So you're with the Government."

She nodded.

I tried a smile, "Which agency?"

Her face was impassive. "I'm with the food and drug administration."

It was an obvious lie and as she continued to stare back at me I knew that she didn't care whether I believed it or not.

"Food and drug," I said. "I didn't think our project would fall under your jurisdiction."

"It does." Without any further explanation she continued, "Shall we get back to the interview?" She opened the file folder again. "You are one of three counsellors?"

I didn't answer.

"Philip Cournvoyer, a psychologist, and Mary Thimple, a third year medical student." She looked up at me again. "What are you currently studying?"

I knew, with a great deal of consternation that the answers to her questions were all in the file so I didn't answer.

She pursed her lips. "You aren't studying anything are you?" Without waiting for my reply she continued. "You aren't a student, a psychologist, or a doctor." She smiled cruelly, "But I see you in a white laboratory coat and as fetching as it is, I wonder why you're wearing it, why you cash a government cheque and what it is exactly that you do here."

I glanced at the thick file and then tried to hold her gaze, "I teach people to dream."

Once again she checked the file, "And how is it that you came to do that? It's not the sort of thing that most people put on a resume."

I could feel my heart beat faster and I was gripped with a fear that had not assailed me since before I met the doctor. The woman in front of me held the power to decide my future. She could make me leave. She could banish me from the sanctuary that was the project.

I swallowed a lump in my throat. "Dr. Storvik hired me…without a resume."

She smirked. "Wouldn't it be closer to the truth to say that Dr. Storvik didn't really hire you but simply acquired your services?"

My voice sounded like a whimper. "I don't know what you mean."

"You used to procure narcotics for the doctor."

I could feel my eyes widen and my mouth opened involuntarily. My hands began to shake.

"Isn't that true, Charlie? You got him dope, didn't you?"

I looked down at my trembling hands. I pressed the clipboard against my lap and fought against the returning pain of the migraine. I closed my eyes and nodded. I couldn't lift my head to see her expression but imagined it to be cold and smug. She would finish me, I thought.

I was surprised when after a few moments of silence the voice that spoke was soft and comforting. "Charlie, look at me."

I looked up, deeply shamed by the tears that I could feel brimming in my eyes.

"This isn't a criminal investigation. You're not in trouble."

I sniffed, trying to control my quickened heart rate before speaking.

She smiled again, but that smile wasn't the chilling charade I saw previously. This was a sunbeam, a dove flying, a gift from Heaven. She closed the file folder again, picked it up and placed it back in the briefcase. She leaned forward on crossed arms and said, "Why don't you tell me how you came to be here. Tell me how you teach people to dream."

I took a deep breath and lowered my head once more. I stared at the clipboard, which now rested lightly on my lap. "I met Dr. Storvik at the library downtown. I was…staying there."

"Staying there?"

I nodded, "It was winter, and during the days I stayed there from open to close."

Her voice was still soft and quiet, "You had been living on the street."

"Yes"

"I'm sorry."

I smiled, "It was a great way to get to know the public library."

She returned the smile, "What did you like to read?"

I could feel myself start to relax. The lingering pain from the migraine disappeared under the caress of her smile. "Lots of things. I started with contemporary literature when I was thirteen. You know, thrillers and mysteries."

Although I knew that information was in the file I was almost shocked by the sympathy in her voice, "You had been on the streets since you were thirteen?"

I nodded slowly, as the comfort of the library was replaced with harsher memories. "My mom died when I was five years old. I never knew my father."

"You didn't have any relatives?"

I shook my head. "I went into a foster home." I paused, "Three actually. Before I made it to a fourth I decided that I could do better on my own."

"I can't imagine how hard it was for you."

I shrugged, "Like I said, it gave me a good chance to catch up on my reading."

"So you never went to school?"

I shook my head, "No, I just kept reading. By the time Dr. Storvik found me, I must have been, oh, seventeen I guess, I was just finishing up the Greek Tragedies." I lifted my chin slightly, "I've read more Classics that Phil and Mary put together."

Her radiant smile banished all traces of nervousness and I continued, "Anyway, that's when Dr. Storvik approached me. He wanted to buy some yellows."

"Yellows?"

"Nembutal." I quickly added, "But not for himself! It was for his research."

"And you got him what he needed."

I nodded, "I knew where to get the stuff so I got it for him."

"What else did you get him?"

"Reds, uh, that's bennies…Benzedrine. DMT, crank, pot, I got him a lot of stuff."

"What about LSD?"

"Yeah, that too, but soon after Dr. Storvik started making all that stuff himself."

"You said he was using it for research, did he make you take any of those drugs?"

I shook my head vehemently, "No, Dr. Storvik only tested those drugs on himself. The only drug that I took was D.E.D. and that was only after the doctor perfected it." I anticipated her next question and said, "D.E.D. stands for Dream Enhancement Drug, or Dream

Enrichment Drug. I can't remember which. It's just what we call it around here, it's not the official name or anything." I paused, "Plus I think Dr. Storvik has a thing for Dedalus. I waited for her smile and when it came I continued. "I began lucid dreaming just by using the doctor's techniques, but after D.E.D… well, it took me well beyond the next level.

She was silent for a moment. "So you were able to achieve a heightened dream state without drugs? No wonder the doctor took you in."

I could hear the defensive tone in my own voice. "The doctor took me in out of kindness." I continued quickly, "I don't have some special gift. Anyone can achieve more lucid dreams if they follow the technique. It just takes practice. I only happened to be the first person that the doctor taught how to do it." I added in a lower voice, "That's my only distinction."

She leaned closer. "I doubt that very much Charlie. I have a feeling there's a lot more to you than meets the eye."

I could feel my cheeks burn crimson and thankfully I didn't have to speak as she pretended not to notice. "Are you really saying that anyone can do it? Anyone can experience it whenever they want?"

I nodded, "That's exactly what I'm saying."

"Once they take the drug."

I shifted in my seat. "It's not just the drug. That only opens your mind to the procedure. The aspect that you can't lose sight of is the exercises, the rituals…" I snapped my fingers, "The programming."

She picked up the pen, "Tell me about the programming."

"Well," I began, "Programming is…well, it's just what the word implies. You program the kind of thoughts that you want to dream about. It's different for everyone but it follows a common thread. Some people react to visuals so they look at pictures or stare at an object to open their thoughts to that specific thing. With other people it's smell, or even taste. Once their minds are focused, which is essentially what D.E.D does, then they can enter the accelerated, or heightened, dream state."

"So they become open to suggestion."

"Well," I shifted in my seat. "They're own suggestions."

She nodded. "Of course, they're own." She smiled, "So what works for you? Which of the five senses do you favour?"

"Um…a combination of things." I added, "But that's the key. You have to find the right combination of touch, taste or whatever. Like I said, everyone's different."

She began to write down some notes in a form of shorthand that I found difficult to decipher. She noticed me leaning forward and stopped writing.

"I like your blouse," I blurted out and immediately feel my cheeks redden.

She smiled, "Thank you." She extended her arm to me. "It's silk."

I reached out tentatively and felt the smooth material between my fingers. The numbness in my lower extremities immediately began and I tapped my feet to shake the feeling off. I mumbled hoarsely, "It's nice."

I let go and looked back down to my lap as I saw her searching my face. After a brief silence she said, "I really appreciate you talking with me Charlie."

She stood up and I followed suit. As we shook hands, I tried not to think about the texture of her skin, lest the numbness begin again.

"I'm sorry I was so stern at first. I've been met with some opposition from the staff here. I don't think my presence here is appreciated by the good doctor."

I said, "Dr. Storvik is very protective of the program."

"With good reason I think." She said with a smile. "After all, this is his baby."

"And his dream." I let out a little laugh, "I mean…"

She laughed, "I knew what you meant."

We lingered in awkward silence and I gave a little shrug. "Well, thank you Miss Hearst."

Her voice dropped to a near whisper. "Madeline."

"Madeline then." My own voice cracked.

She turned to go and my eyes finally swept over the length of her, taking in the minute details of her form. As we left the room she turned to me, "Charlie, be honest with me. How real are the dreams?"

With as much sincerity and solemnity as I could muster I said, "As real as you and I right now."

I watched her walk toward Dr. Storvik's office and did not fight the numbness that began at my feet, encircled my legs and wound its way around my torso. When she was gone I hurried to my room, where in the closet hung a gift from Dr. Storvik, given to me for my birthday two years ago; a silk scarf that I would finally put to use.

The wind on top of the mountain was blowing hard but it wasn't cold. I walked to the edge of the cliff and stared down at the valley below. I leaned forward, easing into the wind and then allowed myself to fall. My arms were spread and my eyes began to water…I stopped them from watering with a blink. I arched my back and felt my descent slow as I levelled out, then I gained altitude, flying over the lush green of the valley, then over a town, then picking up speed I flew over a city and weaved in between buildings. I steered myself to a towering high rise and landed on the penthouse balcony. The sliding glass door gave me a perfect reflection. I was shirtless and tanned, my dark hair highlighted with touches of gold. I smiled at my own reflection, at my straight white teeth, my crystal blue eyes… my muscular arm reached for the door and stepped inside.

Madeline was seated on a cream colored leather sectional. She was dressed in a white silk negligee. "Charlie," she said my name and her voice was full of longing, and desire. She stood up and came to me, her arms around my shoulders, drawing me closer. I bent down to kiss her and her lips were soft and pliant. She moaned against my lips...

I would use that scarf every night for the next two months. I saw Madeline daily, passing her in the hall, or sharing a coffee in the lounge. She and her partner, the dour faced man named Spivins, took a more active part in the project's operations. More "FDA" agents were brought in and although initially I expressed concern over the intrusion, Madeline disarmed my worries with a smile and her soothing words would lull me into a delicious numbness.

It was bliss to have her with me every night. Once my silk scarf was lightly scented with her perfume, the dreams became even more vivid. Every night before bed I would joyfully program her into my dream and each time was better than the last.

I saw little of Dr. Storvik, but each time he appeared, he was all smiles, rushing off to sequester himself in his private laboratory. All was going well, and Donald, who I long considered the most under achieving of all subjects, was making progress at an exponential rate. I had high hopes for him and his own excitement was barely contained. His night time odysseys were becoming intricately woven stories and detail rich adventures.

Philip and Mary were another story however. They were bitter over having to share their research with the new duo from the government. "FDA, what a crock of shit!" Philip hissed to Mary during a lunch break. "What kind of idiots do they think we are?"

Mary leaned forward and spoke in a conspiratorial whisper. "I hear they're CIA. Lucille overheard them yesterday talking about "the agency"."

Philip spat, "That fucking Spivins practically ruined my notes on Subject 8. He tore out sections, highlighted sentences and even spilled coffee on the medication log. Moron!"

Mary's voice was still hushed, "And I personally wouldn't be surprised if Lucille was right, because there's something about those two that really freaks me out. They seem sinister. Plus they dismissed almost all the subjects except the violent offenders. What does that say?"

Philip continued to ignore her. "They can't keep fucking up my notes like that. This is MY research that they're interfering with. The other doctors they brought in won't even consult with me on the tests! They're taking over the loony bin." He drained the coffee from the paper cup he was holding and stood up. "Have either of you seen Storvik?"

I said, "Probably in the lab. He's been in there almost every day for the last month."

Philip made a face, "Figures, is Dr. Frankenstein planning on reanimating the dead now?" I shifted angrily but Mary giggled, "Maybe he's working on a bride for Charlie."

They both laughed and as usual, I beat a hasty retreat.

As soon as I stepped out into the bright glare of the hallway I felt the familiar, crippling pain stab at the back of my neck. I reached into my pocket for the pills but as soon as my hand grasped the bottle I knew it was empty. The last pill had been consumed the previous week. I steadied myself against the wall with my free hand and took three deep breaths. Looking down the hall toward the office I squinted against the light. I started off, desperate for the medication that the doctor kept locked in his desk drawer. My vision started to fail, black spots danced and all images on the periphery blurred to a beige fog. Each footstep sent a stabbing pain upward and I prayed that I wouldn't pass out before I reached the office.

I stumbled over the carpet that marked the beginning of the reception area and once I rounded the corner I saw that Lucille was not at her desk. I went past her workstation and tried the door to the office. A wave of nausea swept over me as the door opened.

Dr. Storvik was at his filing cabinet, peering into the drawer but as soon as he saw me, he realized the state I was in. He was at my side instantly, moving remarkably fast for a man approaching eighty years. He led me to his couch and I collapsed, my vision completely gone and too wracked with pain to turn my thought to this new, frightening affliction. I felt two pills pushed into my palm and after instinctively throwing the double dose to the back of my throat I heard the doctor's voice. "Put them under your tongue!" But it was too late and I felt the acid burn my throat as I began to choke. I swallowed them, retching from the chalky substance. A moment later a glass of water was place in my hand and I greedily drank, causing me to sputter and cough.

The blackness almost immediately shifted and faded, leaving gray patches that swam along the outside of my vision. When two minutes had passed, those too faded and I blinked back tears of relief. The doctor was now sitting across from me, his brow creased with concern.

"They are getting worse, yes?" He asked, his accent as thick as ever. "Are all the pills I gave you gone?"

I nodded, not trusting my voice.

He sighed, "I'm working on this Charlie. Please believe me."

I wiped the tears away on my sleeve, "Did you get the results from the Cat scan?"

"Eh? No, not yet Charlie. But don't worry. Try not to anyway."

I smiled as the paid dripped away with each passing second. "I trust you Dr. Storvik."

He returned the smile, showing his pipe stained dentures. He ran his palms down the front of his corduroy trousers. "Apart from the circumstances, I'm glad to see you Charlie. I wanted to show you something."

He stood up and went over to his desk, opening the top drawer and rummaging around. I said, "I was lucky to find you here.

You've been holed up in the lab for weeks now." He nodded absentmindedly, shuffling papers and other oddments aside. After a few disgusted grunts he extracted a photograph and held it up exultingly. "Found it!" He smiled as he gazed down on it and after a wistful sigh he brought it over to me and I took it from him. It was old, yellowed from age and wrinkled from much handling. It was a picture of two young men, one handsome and stylish in his suit and the other small and bent over, dressed in an ill fitting sweater. They were both smiling, arms around each other's shoulders, standing in front of what appeared to be a museum. I handed it back to him with a shy smile.

"That is me, the handsome devil, and my friend Georg. That picture was taken in Vienna, before the war." He ran his bent finger along the edge as he stared at the photo. "I was young then. Much younger than you are now."

He continued to smile as memories no doubt cascaded over him but soon after the corners of his mouth began to sag and his eyes became shiny with tears. "In Dachau…" He began, but his voice was cracked with emotion and he took a few deep breaths before continuing. "In Dachau, Georg and I were together. Best friends, outside, and best friends inside. He was a lot like you. Small, skinny, like you. Also…" He pointed to my leg, "Lame. Also like you." He sighed deeply. "The guards treated him worse than me. They would beat and taunt him, every day without fail. Towards the end, he couldn't even walk. So they killed him, as we both knew they would. He was strong though! They never killed his spirit! He was the one who taught me to dream. It was that gift that saved me. No matter what atrocity was committed, what evil done, I could escape every night. No fences could hold me and I survived because of that."

He stood up suddenly and put the picture back in the drawer. He looked down at it a moment longer and then he slammed the drawer shut. "I never told anyone what I could do. I let all those other prisoners suffer because I was afraid. I was too afraid of my secret being known, of the Nazis finding out, that I never let anyone else escape." His chest rose with a mighty breath and he continued, "When I got out, I went back to Vienna and studied. I became a doctor. I wanted to help people. I knew it was what I had to do. It was my penance. But I was not forgiven so easily as there are diseases that cannot be cured. There is suffering and pain that is not caused by war, or a virus, or by bacteria. I saw that everyone suffered and I sought to find a cure. I wanted to cure...like. I wanted everyone to be free, to escape the fences of reality. But...besides Georg and I, who could master it? I knew that Georg had a gift and somehow he had given it to me. My research began thirty years ago. I failed, oh, miserably! But I did not give up!" He sighed again. "Perhaps I should have." He looked at me imploringly, "I only wanted to help people."

I almost rose to my feet. "You did doctor! You helped me! You gave me that gift! And the others here too! You found a way to help us!"

He didn't seem to hear me. "When I first saw you in the library, a dirty little urchin...I saw Georg." His tears finally began to fall. "Charlie, I saw your pain! Yes, you helped me immensely, there is no doubt of that, but the bottom line is that I wanted to help you!" I sat immobilized by fear. My savior was crumbling, my hero was weak.

I whispered, "You did help me. You saved me."

He wiped his eyes with the back of his hand and opened the bottom drawer. He withdrew a large bottle of pills and gave them to me. "Take two if you feel the pain begin." He was shaking and he hastily buried his hands in his pockets. "Take three if you must." He turned to the anterior door, "Now Charlie, get some rest. I must get back to the laboratory." He opened the door without another glance and I heard the lock click as he shut it behind him.

I remained in the office, sitting and staring at the wall, trying to absorb this frightful change in the man who was like a father to me. I glanced at my watch and saw that I had two hours until I had to interview Donald. Previous to my meeting with the doctor I had been looking forward to the session because of the rotation I had not seen him in over two weeks. I decided to have a quick nap, as I felt the need to escape to the netherworld like never before. I limped down the hallway, past the guards that were now always to be seen. Four more men in lab coats that I didn't recognize were in front of one of the examination rooms, speaking in hushed tones. I went past more unfamiliar faces before I got to my room. I lay down on the bed and began counting down from one hundred, programming my dream...

Phil lay on the ground, his hand holding his bloody nose. "I'm sorry Charlie, I didn't mean it." Madeline put her arm around my waist and said, "Darling, we should go." We were in a sports car, a black Bugatti Veyron. The speedometer hit 200 miles an hour and Madeline was beside me, laughing. She turned to me, "I love you, Charlie. I love you so much." I leaned over to kiss her but the car began to swerve... I made the car stop swerving. I leaned over, but the car swerved again and then the engine died. I looked at the speedometer and we were slowing down. I turned to Madeline but she was gone. The passenger seat was empty.

I was standing on the side of the road. The car was gone and I was alone. I took a deep breath and decided to fly back to my penthouse. I closed my eyes and saw myself flying but my feet never left the pavement. My mother spoke, "Charlie, I'm sorry. I drank too much and I snorted cocaine. I took acid. I shot heroin. I smoked crack."

"No." I said out loud, forcefully.

"I fucked strangers. I was a whore. I did so many bad things and I'm sorry."

I tried to fly away but I couldn't.

"The doctor said it was fetal alcohol syndrome. They said that I was to blame for what you were."

I ordered a storm to come and wash her away but the sun continued to shine. I wanted the wind to blow the image of my mother away. I screwed my eyes closed and wished her to be gone.

"You lazy, stupid boy!" It was the voice of my first foster mother. I kept my eyes closed.

"You dirty thing! You're nothing but a bug!" I started to run down the highway. I went faster and faster but then my leg started to ache.

"I did that!" It was my foster father. The one who beat me with a baseball bat until my leg was shattered. "I can kill you anytime I want!"

I started to crawl along the road...

I slept too long and was almost twenty minutes late for my session with Donald. I hastily got dressed and made my way out of the near empty west wing.

I stopped at the door to the consulting room but the clipboard was not there. It was one of Lucille's many duties to insure that the files were affixed in time for the interview. Nevertheless, I opened the door and stepped aside.

"About fucking time!" Donald spat as soon as he saw me.

"Sorry Donald. I had a nap and my alarm didn't go off." I sheepishly explained as I sat down.

His grizzled face was twisted in anger. "Isn't that a switch? How about for a change you tell me about your dreams. How were they? How real was it? Did you get to tie Miss April to the bed?"

I was shocked at his uncharacteristic outburst. I stared at him with wide eyes while he glowered at me. His breathing was erratic and I softly asked, "What's going on Donald? Did the nightmares come back?"

He laughed mockingly. "Did the nightmares come back? No, they didn't fucking come back! The nightmare is having to live in this shit hole and get dissected like a fucking guinea pig by you head shrinkers!" He leaned forward suddenly, causing me to recoil.

"I'll tell you what Charlie, the next time that fucking ivy league prick comes in here I'm gonna stab him with this pencil! And if that little bitch Mary comes in, I'll do more than just dream about having my way with her." A chilling smile stretched his lips, "Or maybe I should hold out for the ice queen...Miz Hearst. I bet she'd warm up under the right circumstances. Yessir, with the proper..." He hissed the next word, "Programming."

I was speechless and ready to make a dash for the door. Donald was a snake ready to strike and I knew that if he were to get violent, security would arrive far too late. Donald would have had to be blind to not see my fear and instead of it feeding his anger, his demeanor softened, and he buried his face in his hands.

"Oh man Charlie, I'm sorry. It's not you that I'm mad at."

My voice still quavered. "Who are you mad at?"

All of a sudden his head snapped up, "Who the fuck do you think I'm mad at?" He pointed to the wall behind me, "Those bastards! They're fucking with me Charlie! They're screwing with my mind!"

"Who? Philip? Mary?"

"They want me to suffer! I know what they think of me! They think I'm just some stupid con who they can fuck with!" His hand shot over to the ashtray and picked it up. I ducked just in time as the ashtray shattered against the wall behind me. "Get the fuck out of here!" He got to his feet, lifted the chair above his head and hurled it against the wall. "Get out of here!"

I hit the panic button that was affixed under the table before I backed out of the room. The last sight I saw before the heavy door locked behind me was Donald attempting to lift the table, grunting and swearing in frustration.

In less than a minute, two burly government men were tearing down the hall toward Examination Room B. I was shouting to them to sedate Donald and above all, not to hurt him.

I was too angry to stay to make sure my orders were carried out. I was limping down the hall as fast as I could toward the lounge where I hoped that I could find my colleagues and some answers to Donald's rash behaviour.

Phillip and Mary were not there but two other doctors were, I ignored them and went to Lucille, who was pouring herself a cup of coffee. I lit into her right away, "What the fuck happened to Donald?"

"Who?"

"Donald! Subject 24! I just had a session with him and he was going nuts! What have they done to him?"

"What are you talking about Charlie?"

"They've done something to him!" I turned to the two doctors and glared at them, "What have you done?"

Lucille set the cup down on the counter, spilling coffee over her hand. She cursed softly as she wiped the tepid coffee from her hand with a washcloth. She looked at me calmly and said, "Come to my desk." When we were out of the lunchroom I asked, "Where are Philip and Mary? They're responsible for this!"

She whispered, "Neither of them have had a session with him in over a month. They were taken off his rotation."

The news didn't even sink in before I asked, "Who took them off the rotation?"

She gave me a condescending smirk. "Maybe you should ask you girlfriend."

I narrowed my eyes. "Are you saying Madeline took them off?"

"Oh Charlie, are you really that stupid?"

I leaned against the doorway, suddenly drained. "Where are they? I need to talk to them."

"They're gone." She turned back to me with a sneer. "Your loving Madeline fired them an hour ago."

I was dumbfounded and slumped even more against the doorframe. Lucille walked over to me. "I guess I'm next." She pushed past, "Excuse me Charlie, I think I'm going to go clear out my desk." I heard her voice behind me but I didn't turn to face her. "And Charlie, I'd advise you to do the same."

I tried to absorb the shocking reality that I too could be gone and the prospect gripped me with fear. I looked around blankly as the seed of panic took root. I cast furtive glances up and down the hall, as if waiting for doom to fall. I expected to see Madeline appear, ready to strike me down. I took a shaky breath and tried to suppress the anxiety that might trigger another migraine. I needed to find Madeline first and plead my case so I traveled down the hallway, looking in every room.

After a fruitless journey through the lounge and even into the empty dorms I made my way back to the west wing, limping painfully. When hope was stretched thin, I saw Madeline, and all I felt was desperation. She was speaking with Spivins, and judging by the body language, she was either giving orders or berating him.

I called out to her as soon as I burst through the glass double doors but she only gave me an irritated glance before turning back to Spivins. When I was about ten yards from her she finally addressed me. "Not now Charlie. I'm very busy."

I kept on, my right leg sending flashes of pain to my midsection. "What's going on Madeline? Please tell me!"

"What do you mean?" She asked icily.

"I heard about Philip and Mary."

She said to Spivins, "I'll catch up to you. You can start without me."

Her partner smirked at me and then left the way that I had come. Madeline also began to walk away briskly in the opposite direction. She didn't turn to face me. "Well? Are you coming?"

I had to trot behind her to keep up and I began to wheeze, "Please stop Madeline!"

She kept on. "If you want to talk, then talk."

My leg was burning and each step made me wince. I needed her to soothe my fears but the words did not come. Her pace increased, "Well? Nothing to say?"

I was now five feet behind her and my leg gave out. I fell, trying in vain to hold onto the wall. I cried out, "Madeline, please!"

She stopped, turned and looked down at me with disgust. I tried to rise to my knees but the poorly knit joint would not cooperate. I stumbled again and looked up at her. "Are you going to make me leave?"

She narrowed her eyes, "What?"

Amidst my shame and fear another migraine took shape and I wished for death, rather than letting her see me completely unmanned. I swallowed back the bile that crept up my throat and felt hot tears in my eyes. "I don't have anywhere else to go!"

I squeezed my eyes shut and her pitiless voice stabbed me. "Get up."

With one hand against the wall I struggled to get back to my feet. I started toward her slowly and her fingers dug into my upper arm, "Come on. You need your rest."

As we walked I tried to open the bottle of pills but when Madeline saw, she snatched it away. "Don't worry Charlie, I'll take care of you."

By the time we reached my room, the black spots had grown and my vision was rapidly fading. I fell onto the bed and twisted onto my side, my hand almost curled into a claw as I reached out to her, "Please…I need those pills."

"Aw, has my baby got a headache?" She crooned.

I clutched the air feebly, "Please!"

Her face was a blur but I felt her hand push me onto my back. "You pathetic little bitch."

I heard her snap the lid of the bottle and I felt two pills being pushed into my palm. I didn't hesitate a moment as I chewed them desperately. I let out a breath of sweet relief despite the pain and I felt her fingers on my lips, "More?" She asked.

I shook my head but two more pills were in my mouth and she tilted my head back roughly and with her other hand massaged my throat until the pills were consumed. The pain began to recede and as I opened my eyes I saw Madeline holding a glass of water out of me.

"You should wash those down." She said as she poured the water over my face, into my mouth, and over my chin. She put the empty glass on the table next to my bed and sat down beside me. "What have we here?" She said as she picked up the bottle of D.E.D that I kept by my bedside. She snickered, "It seems like the good doctor has no reservations about handing out dope." She uncapped the lid and held one against my lips.

"Take it, you want to have pleasant dreams don't you?" I tried to shake my head but the pain from the migraine left me crippled and as weak as a baby. She put the pill in my mouth and I had no choice but to swallow it. She held another pill between her index finger and thumb, moving it across my line of sight. "Of course, Dr. Storvik never did have any problems with giving you drugs." She put the pill on my lips but I managed to spit it out. She slapped me twice, "Bad boy! Won't take his medicine!" She took another pill out of the bottle and pressed it into my mouth.

I closed my eyes but she slapped me again, "Stay with me Charlie. You have a right to know about that pillar of virtue, that savior of mankind who you worship."

I watched her through half closed eyes and I checked the numbness that crept up my legs. "He doped you from the beginning Charlie. All those narcotics you bought for him ended up inside you. First he'd knock you out with some yellows and then drop a tab of acid on your tongue." I shook my head but she only laughed. "He slipped PCP into your porridge, he but DMT in your spaghetti-o's. He made so many chemical milkshakes that he made Timothy Leary look like a kid with a chemistry set." She laughed. "What a friend that doctor is! What a pal!" With mock sympathy in her voice she said, "He used you Charlie. But you weren't his first guinea pig." She smiled cruelly, "Did the doctor tell you he was a prisoner at

Dachau?" Her smile grew, "I see that he did. Well, he was there anyway. That part is true." She leaned close to my ear and whispered, "He killed a lot of people trying to perfect his drug."

I felt a tear leak from my eye and it stung, all the way down my cheek. Madeline looked away in disgust and her eyes fell on the silk scarf that I had been keeping next to my pills for the past two months. She picked it up and held it to her face. "Chanel." The sweetest smile imaginable came to her face and she brought the scarf down to me and drew its softness across my cheek. "You dreamt about me didn't you?" As the silk went from my cheek to my lips she cooed, "What did you dream about?" She drew the scarf lightly across my lips. "Was I good Charlie? I bet I was." Suddenly she stuffed the scarf into my mouth. "Suck on that, you pervert." The bed creaked as she stood up. "Sweet dreams Charlie."

I was too weak to move and the numbness continued to travel up my body. I fought back shame as all her words became gospel. I was sick. I was a pervert. I was pathetic. No, those were her words, her suggestions, her programming. I reached up and ripped the scarf out of my mouth but lacked the strength to cast it away. I filled my mind with hate, with thoughts of violence and cruelty against her so when I fell asleep, I could make those thoughts become reality.

I'd played the hero so many nights. I was the perfect lover. I fought like a hero. I danced, because at night I could be anything I wanted to be. My leg wasn't smashed in a foster home, clubbed by a drunken man. My teeth were white and straight, not crooked and gapped from a lead pipe wielding drug dealer. I had to be strong and handsome, because Fate had been cruel to me and dealt disfigurement and weakness for the waking hours. I lived at night, in full color, stereo sound, true as life detail. I played the hero, and sometimes, I played the villain too.

All my foster parents were in a courtyard. They wore rags and they were lined up and afraid. A guard was walking behind them. He wore a Nazi uniform. He held up a gun and shot each one in the back of the head. One by one they dropped. The guard smiled. It was Dr. Storvik.

My room was dark when I awoke with a start. The clock's red lights told me that I had slept long into the night. I still felt weak and I heard breathing that was not my own. I lay completely still and before I could wonder if my mind was still in a dream, a deep voice spoke. "Are you awake Charlie?"

I couldn't place the voice immediately but when he spoke again, I knew it was Donald.

"I wish you would go back to sleep. It would make this a lot easier."

I reached for the light switch. "Donald?"

"Don't turn the light on!"

My hand jerked back. "What are you doing here?"

He didn't answer right away. "I killed them Charlie."

"They can't hurt you Donald. It's just a nightmare."

"No!" He yelled, "Not them!" He took a breath and let it out slowly. "I killed the doctor. I killed Philip." He drew another deep breath. "I killed Mary."

"Did you hear me?" He asked when I didn't reply.

"I heard you."

"Well, good. I'm glad you heard me."

"Why? Why did you do it?"

"I had to! I just knew it was what I had to do! Don't you ever do things without knowing why?"

I thought he was delusional and tried to believe that it was just a lucid dream. "When did you do it?"

"Tonight."

"How did you get out of the dorm? Didn't security stop you?"

"I know what you're thinking. You think I dreamt it."

"Sometimes, when you reach the heightened dream state the line becomes blurred and it takes some adjustment..."

"Shut up! Just shut up! It was real! There were no guards! You know they moved me to a private room two weeks ago!"

"Who moved you Donald?"

"The woman! She moved me!"

I licked my lips. "Madeline?"

"Who else?"

"Donald, try to think now. Has she been...um...suggesting things to you?"

His voice sank to a whisper. "Stop talking Charlie. Just shut up now." I heard the floor creak as he shifted position. "I have to do it. I like you. You were the only one that was nice to me here. I'm so sorry."

I could feel the hairs on the back of my neck stand up. "What do you have to do Donald?"

I heard a metallic click. "I have to kill you."

I could hear the fear in my voice. "No Donald. You don't have to do anything you don't want to."

He started to cry. "Yes I do. I always have to do what I don't want to do! I always..."

His voice broke off in sobs.

"Don't do this."

He continued to cry and I began to measure the distance from the bed to the crack of light under the door.

"I'm your friend Donald."

The bed creaked as I tried to get my legs over the edge of the bed. I slowly let my left leg drop as his cries grew louder. The bed creaked again as is shifted my weight.

"Donald?"

More sobs.

"Donald?"

Silence.

I waited for the span of five heartbeats. "Donald?"

Suddenly there was a flash of light and the deafening sound of a gunshot. I dove for the floor, expecting the pain to hit me at any second. When it never came I lay face down, taking deep breaths, not daring to move. "Donald?" Something warm and wet touched my right hand. "Are you alright?"

When no answer came I stood up and tentatively stepped over to the light switch and turned it on. I saw the blood on my hand and on the light switch. I whirled around to see Donald's body, lying in a twisted heap on the floor, an island in a pool of blood. The head was misshapen, the face destroyed. I turned away in revulsion and threw up over the nightstand, covering the pills and sending them tumbling to the floor.

I knelt by the bed for what seemed like an eternity, drawing deep breaths. When I stood up the room began to spin and I shut my eyes, preparing for another migraine. When it didn't come I opened my eyes, knelt down beside the body of my former friend and took the gun from his bloody hand.

With the weapon held firmly in my right hand I walked down the corridor and turned into the main hallway, toward Dr. Storvik's office. I knew that at any moment one of the government flunkies could appear but I didn't care. I'd kill them without remorse, without thought, without any flicker of regret. But no one came. I made it to the doctor's sanctuary unscathed.

The office was dark but the light under the back door told me that the doctor was in the lab. I stepped to the door, tried it, and found that it was locked. I banged on the door with the butt of the gun. "Dr. Storvik! Let me in!"

When no answer came I took a step back, pointed the fun at the lock and fired. I missed hitting the frame, so I fired again. The bullet sent up sparks when it hit the lock and the door opened an inch or two from the impact. I pushed it open and stepped inside.

The lab had been cleared of all the doctor's things. Two long rows of counters stood bare and lying between them was the doctor. I didn't go to him because I knew he was dead. The pool of blood was wide around his body, as if he had been made of nothing else.

"Oh Charlie, don't look." Madeline's soft voice spoke behind me. "It'll give you nightmares."

I turned, pointing the gun at her chest.

She laughed, "Put that down, silly. You can't shoot me."

She walked around me to the counter and leaned against it nonchalantly. I kept the gun on her but I felt my hand begin to shake.

"You don't look good Charlie." She giggled, "Maybe you should take a nap."

She laughed, "Well, aren't you going to ask me why? Aren't you going to curse me?" She titled her head to the side. "Where's the righteous indignation? Don't you even have the balls to raise your voice to me?"

I shook my head. "I don't have anything to say." I squeezed the trigger and the gun went off. The filing cabinet behind Madeline shook. I had missed. I pulled the trigger again. Click.

Her mouth was open in shock. "You little prick! You were actually going to shoot me!"

She took two steps toward me and slapped my face. I raise the empty gun to hit her but her hand clamped down on my wrist and held me back. She squeezed and twisted until the gun dropped and then she pushed me to the floor. "You pathetic weakling!" She hissed as she picked up the gun.

She held the gun out and released the empty clip and then reached into her purse and took out a magazine, snapping it into place professionally. She pointed the gun at me, "Stand up."

After I got to my feet she motioned to me with the gun, "Into the office, I want to show you something."

I backed in, keeping my eyes on the gun, and away from her perfect face.

On the doctor's desk was a thick file folder. She picked it up with her free hand. "Sit down."

I let myself sink onto the couch and she sat on top of the desk, facing me. She opened the file. "This is the biggest file the doctor had. Guess who it belongs to."

I remained silent.

She smirked, holding up the folder to me. "Charlie Graves, guinea pig, gimp, and all around nice guy."

She held it loosely, "What secrets do you want to know?" When I didn't reply she gleefully held up an image of my what I assumed to be my brain. "How about those nasty headaches of yours?" She pointed to the back of the cranium. "See this dark patch here. Well that's one mother of a tumor. It seems that wonder drug D.E.D has a couple of nasty side effects." She put the X-ray back in the folder and smiled. "Dry mouth, nausea, and oh yeah, death." She shook her head sadly, "I'm sorry to tell you this Charlie, but you don't have much time left." She put the folder down beside her. "I tried to give you a much quicker death but that Donald has trouble following instructions. Kill Charlie, THEN kill yourself." She laughed,

"Maybe I wasn't clear enough." She winked, "I'll know better next time."

"So," I said after clearing my throat. "This is what the project was to you. A place to get cheap assassins. You give them some D.E.D, whisper some instructions and then..." I summoned a smile, just like I did in my dreams when I defeated the villain. "Must save a bundle on training. A homeless guy or an ex con is a lot easier to work with than some disgruntled Green Beret. When the job is done they just blow their own brains out." I snapped my fingers. "Or maybe you think you can drop a pill in some CEO's drink and get him to hand over a million bucks. Maybe you could drug the President or some dictator...then you guys can dictate foreign policy from the inside out. Or do you want a few bombs dropped? Wait! I know! You can drop it in the drinking water and get everyone to drink whatever soft drink you invested in."

Her mouth became rigid. "Those are all great ideas. I think any one of those would be a much better use of the drug. More profitable than giving people pleasant dreams."

"Yeah," I said, "You would think that."

"Yes Charlie, I would. You see, unlike you, I have a life. I can go out and get laid for real. I can live my life when I'm awake."

She pointed the gun at me, "Let's go for a walk, Igor." She picked up the folder and tucked it under her arm. We both stood and she directed me down the hallway. "Let's get you back to your room."

As we walked she said, "I do wonder though, how close was the doctor? Do you think he could have found a cure for you? What about the other thirty-one subjects? That crazy bastard was on his way to mass murder with all those cute little tumors out there. At least they'll go peacefully in a mental hospital." After a few more steps she said. "Would it have a made a difference to you? Knowing I mean. Would you have still taken D.E.D knowing that it was going to kill you?"

I didn't answer. I stumbled against the wall.

"I guess it doesn't really matter." She prodded me in the back with the gun. "Come on Charlie, relief is a few more steps away."

I went on for another two or three paces and then collapsed to my knees, leaning my palms onto the cold tile floor.

"Get up!" She commanded, pushing the gun to my head.

I took a deep breath and made an effort to stand but I fell back to my knees. "Get up you cripple! Get up!" She gripped me under the arm and tried to lift me. The folder fell to the ground and a few pages spilled out from the file. "Shit!" She exerted more force to lift me and then, when I judged her face was close enough, I shot out my elbow and almost smiled as it connected with her nose.

She fell back and I was on top of her in a flash, pinning the hand that held the gun to the floor. Blood streamed out of her once perfect nose and I slammed my head down against her face. She let out a grunt and the gun was loose. I head butted her again and grasped the gun while rolling free of her flailing legs.

I got to my feet quickly and pointed the gun at her. She snarled, "Killing me won't solve anything. All the research notes are miles away now. We've got everything we need." She laughed, and blood poured out of her mouth. "You're not asleep Charlie. You can't save the world."

I frowned. "I know. I can only save myself."

She sneered. "You can't kill me. You don't have the…"

I pulled the trigger.

The shot echoed down the hallway and the smell of gunpowder was acrid in my nostrils. I fired again, but there was no need. I tucked the gun into my pants and picked up the file, stuffing the errant papers back inside. Then, as the doctor would say, I danced down the hall, and out into the world.

Made in the USA
San Bernardino, CA
23 November 2019